Published 2024

Printed in the United States of America

First Edition
ISBN (softcover): 978-1-963380-25-5
ISBN (e-book): 978-1-963380-26-2

For information, address:
Holzer Books LLC
8 The Green, Ste. A
Dover, Delaware 19901 USA

For information about special discounts available for bulk purchases, sales promotions, and educational needs, contact:
info@holzerbooksllc.com
+1 (888) 901-7776

holzerbooksLLC©

Chapter 1

Georgiy Sergeyevich Garbuz stood at the center of his office. At forty-one years old, his presence commanded respect, matched only by his intellectual prowess. The bustling research institute surrounding him was a testament to his dedication to innovation and discovery.

His office was a sanctuary of brilliance. The walls were adorned with awards and certificates recognizing his contributions to various fields of science. Shelves overflowed with meticulously organized books and journals, showcasing his breadth of knowledge in astrophysics, biotechnology, and space exploration. Each item in the room was a piece of his journey, a testament to his relentless pursuit of knowledge.

A large desk dominated the room, cluttered with papers, prototypes of futuristic gadgets, and a holographic display projecting complex equations and diagrams. Georgiy's fingers moved deftly over the holographic interface, adjusting variables and tweaking designs for his latest project. The walls were lined with concept art of space colonies and visionary projects he dreamed of realizing, each one a step toward a future he believed humanity could achieve.

GEORGIY SERGEYEVICH GARBUZ

Above his desk hung a banner that read, "Za Detey - For Kids! Za Lyubov - For Love." The simple, yet profound motto served as a constant reminder of his guiding principles. For Georgiy, these words encapsulated his life's mission: to create a better world for future generations and to do so with compassion and empathy.

His gaze often drifted to the banner, drawing strength and inspiration from its message. "Za Detey - For Kids!" This part of the motto reminded him that his work was not just about advancing technology but about ensuring that the next generation inherited a world filled with opportunities and hope. He envisioned space colonies where children could grow up exploring the cosmos, learning and thriving in environments that pushed the boundaries of human potential.

"Za Lyubov - For Love," echoed through his mind, reminding him that at the heart of all scientific endeavor must be a genuine care for humanity. This love drove him to create technologies that would improve lives, heal the sick, and bridge the gaps between people. It was this compassion that fueled his desire to see humanity united, reaching for the stars together.

Georgiy paused, his gaze drifting to a particular piece of concept art—a sprawling space colony orbiting a distant planet. He smiled, imagining the possibilities. His mind raced with ideas, each more ambitious than the last. He had dedicated his life to pushing the boundaries of what was possible, and he wasn't about to stop now.

His thoughts were interrupted by a knock on the door. Turning, he saw his assistant, Natalia, standing in the doorway. Her eyes sparkled with excitement, a reflection of the energy that filled the institute.

"Georgiy, the board meeting is about to start," Natalia said, her voice tinged with anticipation. "They're eager to hear about your latest findings."

Georgiy nodded, straightening his tie and smoothing out his lab coat. "Thank you, Natalia. I'll be right there."

As he followed her down the corridor, Georgiy's mind continued to churn with ideas. The institute buzzed with activity, researchers and scientists moving purposefully through the halls, each one working on their own slice of the future. Georgiy took a deep breath, feeling a surge of pride. He had built this place from the ground up, and it was thriving.

Chapter 2

Entering the boardroom, Georgiy was greeted by the eager faces of the institute's board members. They were a diverse group, each one a leader in their respective field, and they all looked to Georgiy for inspiration.

"Good morning, everyone," Georgiy began, his voice steady and confident. "I'm excited to share with you the progress we've made on our latest project. As you know, our goal is to develop sustainable space colonies, and I'm pleased to report that we've made significant strides."

He activated the holographic display, and the room filled with projections of his designs. The board members leaned forward, their interest palpable. Georgiy walked them through the advancements they had made, explaining the intricacies of the propulsion systems and the innovative materials they were developing.

"This is just the beginning," Georgiy concluded. "With continued support and collaboration, I believe we can achieve something truly extraordinary. The future of humanity lies beyond our planet, and it's up to us to make that future a reality."

The room erupted in applause, and Georgiy felt a swell of satisfaction. But he knew there was still much work to be done. As the meeting adjourned, he returned to his office, his mind already racing with new ideas and improvements.

Back at his desk, Georgiy picked up a small prototype of a device he had been working on. It was a miniature model of a propulsion system, designed to be more efficient and sustainable than anything currently in use. He turned it over in his hands, lost in thought.

His office door opened, and Natalia entered, carrying a stack of papers. "Georgiy, these are the latest research papers you requested."

"Thank you, Natalia," he said, accepting the documents. "I'll review them immediately."

As she left, Georgiy returned to his work, immersing himself in the data. Hours passed in a blur of calculations and revisions. The sun set outside, casting long shadows across his office, but Georgiy barely noticed. He was consumed by his vision, driven by a relentless desire to push the boundaries of human knowledge.

Finally, as the night grew late, Georgiy leaned back in his chair, his eyes weary but his mind still racing. He glanced at the banner on his wall one last time before closing his eyes. Tomorrow was a new day, and there was still so much to do. The future awaited, and Georgiy Sergeyevich Garbuz was determined to lead humanity into it, one groundbreaking discovery at a time.

Chapter 3

The next morning, Georgiy awoke with a renewed sense of purpose. He had always felt the weight of his responsibilities, but today was different. Today, he would be presenting his life's work to the world, sharing his vision for humanity's future beyond Earth.

His office was already a hive of activity. Natalia was busy organizing his travel documents and ensuring that everything was in order for his departure. Georgiy moved methodically, packing his suitcase with meticulous care. He double-checked that he had all the necessary documents, research papers, and prototypes he needed for the conference.

"Georgiy, I've confirmed your flight details and your accommodations at the conference hotel," Natalia said, handing him a printed itinerary. "You have a packed schedule, but I've made sure there's time for you to meet with some key figures in the field."

"Thank you, Natalia," Georgiy replied, glancing up from his suitcase. "This conference is crucial. Our work on sustainable space colonies could change the future of humanity. It's important we get this right."

He carefully packed his research papers and prototypes, his mind wandering to the potential impact of his work. He envisioned a future where humanity had expanded beyond Earth, living in harmony with advanced technologies that made life better for all. His presentation included detailed models of propulsion systems that could make interstellar travel more efficient and sustainable, as well as innovative designs for space habitats that could support human life on distant planets.

Natalia interrupted his thoughts with an email notification. "Georgiy, you have a message from Dr. Li. He's reviewing the final draft of your presentation slides."

Georgiy opened the email and quickly scanned through Dr. Li's comments. They were thorough and insightful, highlighting areas that could be clarified or expanded upon. Georgiy made a few last-minute adjustments, ensuring his presentation was as compelling as possible.

Satisfied, he closed his laptop and placed it in his bag. "Natalia, everything looks good. I think we're ready."

She smiled, her excitement mirroring his own. "I'll arrange for your car to the airport. You're going to do great, Georgiy."

He nodded, appreciating her confidence in him. "Thank you, Natalia. Let's make this conference one to remember."

The drive to the airport was filled with a sense of anticipation. As the car weaved through the city's bustling streets, Georgiy's mind was a whirlwind of thoughts. He mentally rehearsed his presentation, fine-tuning his delivery and anticipating questions from the audience. This was his chance to not only showcase his work but to inspire others to join him in his quest for a better future.

At the airport, he moved through security quickly, his focus unwavering. He spotted several familiar faces in the terminal—colleagues and fellow scientists, all heading to the same conference. They greeted each other with nods and smiles, a shared sense of purpose uniting them.

Boarding the plane, Georgiy found his seat and settled in. He pulled out his tablet, reviewing his notes one last time. The cabin filled with the quiet murmur of conversations, the excitement of the passengers palpable. Georgiy joined in eagerly, sharing anecdotes from his research and discussing the potential of sustainable space colonies.

As the plane taxied down the runway, Georgiy felt a surge of determination. This conference was more than just a platform for his ideas—it was a stepping stone toward a future where humanity could thrive among the stars. He closed his eyes, picturing the space colonies he had designed, bustling with life and innovation.

Chapter 4

As Georgiy settled into his seat, he noticed a familiar face across the aisle. Dr. Patel, a renowned astrophysicist, waved and made his way over to Georgiy's seat.

"Georgiy! It's good to see you," Dr. Patel said, extending his hand. "Are you ready for the conference?"

"Absolutely, Raj," Georgiy replied, shaking his hand firmly. "I'm looking forward to discussing our latest findings and hearing about the advancements in your research."

As they conversed, more scientists boarded the plane, and the cabin buzzed with intellectual energy. Georgiy recognized many colleagues, each one a leader in their field. The atmosphere was charged with excitement and anticipation.

Dr. Yang, a biotechnologist who had made significant strides in regenerative medicine, took the seat next to Georgiy. "Georgiy, it's always a pleasure," she said with a warm smile. "I've heard about your recent work on sustainable space habitats. I can't wait to hear more about it."

"Thank you, Mei," Georgiy replied. "I've been following your research as well. Your breakthroughs in tissue regeneration are nothing short of revolutionary."

As the plane continued to fill, conversations flowed freely among the scientists. They shared updates on their work, exchanged ideas, and speculated about the future of their respective fields. Georgiy felt a sense of camaraderie with his peers, knowing they were all united by a common goal: to push the boundaries of human knowledge and improve life on Earth and beyond.

The flight attendants began their pre-flight announcements, and the scientists gradually settled into their seats. Georgiy glanced around the cabin, noting the focused expressions on his colleagues' faces. Each one was a pioneer in their field, driven by a relentless curiosity and a desire to make a difference.

As the plane taxied down the runway, Dr. Patel leaned over to Georgiy. "You know, this conference feels different," he said. "There's a sense of urgency, as if we're on the brink of something truly groundbreaking."

Georgiy nodded. "I feel it too. The advancements we've made in the past few years are extraordinary, and I believe we're about to enter a new era of scientific discovery."

The plane lifted off smoothly, and Georgiy looked out the window at the receding cityscape. As the ground disappeared from view, he felt a surge of determination. This conference was an opportunity to share his vision and inspire others to join him in his quest for a better future.

Throughout the flight, Georgiy continued to engage in discussions with his colleagues. They debated the feasibility of interstellar travel, the ethical implications of genetic engineering, and the potential for artificial intelligence to revolutionize various industries. Each conversation left Georgiy more energized and motivated.

Midway through the flight, Dr. Yang brought up a topic that had been on Georgiy's mind. "Georgiy, what do you think about the potential for space colonies to address overpopulation and resource depletion on Earth?"

Georgiy leaned back in his seat, considering her question. "I believe space colonies could be a viable solution, but they must be designed with sustainability in mind. We need to ensure that these habitats can support human life without depleting the resources of the planets they inhabit. It's a complex challenge, but one we must tackle if we want to secure a future for humanity."

Dr. Yang nodded thoughtfully. "You're right. And it's not just about survival—it's about creating environments where people can thrive and reach their full potential."

Their conversation continued, touching on various aspects of space colonization and the technological advancements needed to make it a reality. Georgiy felt a deep sense of satisfaction knowing that his work was contributing to these critical discussions.

As the plane began its descent, the scientists prepared for their arrival. Georgiy packed away his tablet and took a deep breath, feeling a mix of excitement and anticipation. This conference was a pivotal moment in his career, and he was ready to make the most of it.

Chapter 5

As the plane reached cruising altitude, the seatbelt sign turned off, and the scientists relaxed into their seats. The cabin crew moved down the aisles, offering refreshments, but most of the passengers were too engrossed in their conversations to notice.

Georgiy sipped his coffee, glancing around at his colleagues. The buzz of conversation was invigorating. He could hear snippets of discussions about everything from quantum computing to the latest breakthroughs in renewable energy.

Dr. Patel leaned over again. "Georgiy, have you heard about Dr. Kwan's recent work on magnetic field shielding for spacecraft? It's supposed to be a game-changer for long-duration space travel."

"I have," Georgiy replied. "It's fascinating work. I've been exploring similar concepts for our propulsion systems. If we can effectively shield against cosmic radiation, it could open up a lot of possibilities for interstellar missions."

As they spoke, a flight attendant approached with a smile. "Gentlemen, would you care for a snack or a drink?"

Dr. Patel waved her off with a polite smile. "No, thank you. We're good for now."

The attendant nodded and moved on, and the conversation resumed. Georgiy felt a sense of camaraderie with his peers, a shared enthusiasm for the possibilities that lay ahead.

The discussions continued throughout the flight, each exchange deepening Georgiy's conviction that they were on the brink of something extraordinary. The collective knowledge and passion in that cabin were palpable, and Georgiy couldn't help but feel optimistic about the future.

Dr. Yang joined their conversation, bringing her unique perspective on biotechnology and its applications in space. "Imagine the possibilities if we could develop self-sustaining ecosystems on Mars," she said. "It would revolutionize agriculture and resource management."

Georgiy nodded. "It's an exciting prospect. And it's not just about survival. We need to create environments where people can thrive. That's why I've been focusing on integrating advanced biotechnology with our habitat designs."

As the plane began its descent, the conversations started to wind down. Georgiy packed away his tablet and took a moment to reflect on the discussions he had had during the flight. Each one had been a reminder of why he was so passionate about his work and why this conference was so important.

The landing was smooth, and soon they were taxiing to the gate. Georgiy looked out the window, catching a glimpse of the bustling airport. He felt a surge of anticipation. This was it—the moment he had been preparing for.

As the plane came to a stop, the scientists gathered their belongings and prepared to disembark. Georgiy joined the queue, exchanging final thoughts with Dr. Patel and Dr. Yang.

"Good luck with your presentation, Georgiy," Dr. Yang said, giving him an encouraging smile. "I have no doubt it will be a highlight of the conference."

"Thank you, Mei," Georgiy replied. "I look forward to hearing your talk as well. We've got an exciting few days ahead of us."

The scientists exited the plane and made their way through the terminal, still chatting animatedly. The sense of shared purpose and camaraderie was strong, and Georgiy felt a renewed sense of determination. This conference was more than just a platform for his ideas—it was an opportunity to inspire and be inspired, to collaborate and push the boundaries of what was possible.

As he stepped into the bright airport terminal, Georgiy took a deep breath. The future awaited, and he was ready to seize it.

Chapter 6

The plane cruised smoothly at 35,000 feet, the gentle hum of the engines providing a backdrop to the lively conversations that filled the cabin. Georgiy leaned back in his seat, thoroughly engaged in a discussion with Dr. Patel and Dr. Yang.

"The potential for using quantum entanglement for instantaneous communication is fascinating," Dr. Patel was saying. "Imagine the implications for space exploration. We could communicate with colonies on Mars or even further in real-time."

Georgiy nodded thoughtfully. "It's a revolutionary idea, but we're still facing significant technical challenges. The stability of quantum states over long distances is a major hurdle. But if we can overcome that, the benefits would be immense."

Dr. Yang chimed in, her eyes sparkling with enthusiasm. "I've been working on integrating biotechnological advancements into space habitat designs. We could create living environments that adapt to the needs of their inhabitants, using bioengineered plants to provide oxygen and recycle waste."

Georgiy smiled. "That's the kind of holistic thinking we need. Sustainability is key if we're going to make long-term space colonization viable."

Around them, other groups of scientists were deep in their own discussions. Georgiy could hear snippets of conversations about the latest developments in artificial intelligence, renewable energy, and advanced propulsion systems. The cabin was a microcosm of the cutting-edge research driving humanity's push towards the stars.

Dr. Patel leaned closer, lowering his voice slightly. "I've also been following the advancements in magnetic field shielding for spacecraft. If we can perfect that technology, it would significantly reduce the risks posed by cosmic radiation on long-duration missions."

Georgiy nodded. "That's critical. Protecting our astronauts is paramount. I'm incorporating some of those ideas into our propulsion systems to ensure they're as safe and efficient as possible."

The conversation flowed seamlessly, each scientist contributing their expertise and insights. Georgiy felt a deep sense of camaraderie and shared purpose. They were all driven by the same goal: to expand humanity's horizons and ensure a sustainable future for generations to come.

As they continued to discuss their work, the flight attendants moved through the cabin, offering drinks and snacks. Georgiy accepted a cup of coffee, taking a moment to savor the rich aroma. He glanced out the window at the endless expanse of sky, feeling a surge of determination.

The future they were working towards was within reach, and he was proud to be part of it.

Dr. Yang took a sip of her tea and turned to Georgiy. "What about you, Georgiy? What are you most excited to share at the conference?"

Georgiy smiled, his eyes lighting up with passion. "I'm presenting our latest research on sustainable space colonies. We've made significant strides in developing propulsion systems that are not only efficient but also environmentally friendly. Our goal is to create self-sustaining habitats that can support human life on distant planets without depleting their resources."

Dr. Patel's eyes widened. "That's incredible. The implications for future space missions are enormous. You're not just thinking about getting us there, but ensuring we can thrive once we arrive."

"Exactly," Georgiy said. "It's about creating a future where humanity can explore the stars sustainably and responsibly. And this conference is the perfect platform to share these ideas and collaborate with others who are just as passionate about pushing the boundaries of what's possible."

The conversations continued, each exchange fueling Georgiy's excitement and resolve. As the plane continued its journey, he felt more confident than ever that they were on the cusp of something truly extraordinary.

Chapter 7

The plane flew steadily through the stratosphere, but as the conversations continued to flow, a sudden jolt interrupted the calm. The cabin lights flickered, and a murmur of concern rippled through the passengers.

Georgiy looked up, his eyes meeting those of Dr. Patel and Dr. Yang. "What was that?" Dr. Patel asked, his voice tinged with unease.

Before Georgiy could respond, the plane lurched again, more violently this time. The seatbelt sign illuminated with a sharp ding, and the captain's voice crackled over the intercom. "Ladies and gentlemen, we are experiencing some unexpected turbulence. Please return to your seats and fasten your seatbelts. We are adjusting our course to navigate through the storm safely. Thank you for your patience."

Georgiy tightened his seatbelt and glanced out the window. The once clear sky was now filled with dark, ominous clouds, and flashes of lightning illuminated the turbulent air. The plane dipped and swayed, each movement sending a jolt of fear through the cabin.

Dr. Yang gripped the armrests of her seat, her knuckles white. "This doesn't feel like ordinary turbulence," she said, her voice barely above a whisper.

Georgiy nodded, his own anxiety rising. He had flown through storms before, but there was something particularly unsettling about this one. The plane's violent movements were accompanied by a strange, low hum that seemed to reverberate through the cabin.

As the turbulence intensified, the flight attendants hurried to secure loose items and reassure passengers. Georgiy's mind raced with both excitement and apprehension. He knew that air travel came with risks, but he couldn't shake the feeling that this was more than just a passing storm.

A particularly violent jolt caused the overhead compartments to rattle, and Georgiy heard the sound of luggage shifting above. The cabin lights flickered again, casting eerie shadows across the worried faces of his fellow passengers.

Dr. Patel leaned over, his voice tense. "Do you think this could be related to the experimental propulsion systems some of the other scientists are working on?"

Georgiy shook his head. "It's unlikely. This feels like a natural phenomenon. But it's definitely strange."

The plane continued to bounce and sway, each lurch intensifying the tension in the cabin. Georgiy's thoughts wandered to the banner in his office: "Za Detey - For Kids! Za Lyubov - For Love." The words echoed in his mind, a reminder of his mission and the future he was striving to create. This turbulence was just another obstacle to overcome, a test of resilience and determination.

Suddenly, a deafening crack of thunder shook the plane, and the cabin was plunged into total darkness. The plane dropped violently, sending a jolt of fear through everyone on board. Oxygen masks deployed from the ceiling, and passengers scrambled to put them on amidst the chaos.

Georgiy's heart pounded in his chest as he fumbled with his mask. The plane continued to plummet, and the shrill sound of alarms filled the cabin. Panicked voices rose above the din, and Georgiy struggled to stay calm. He felt an intense pressure building in his ears, and the sensation of freefall was overwhelming.

"Brace for impact!" the captain's voice shouted over the intercom, but it was barely audible over the cacophony of fear and chaos.

Georgiy gripped the armrests, his knuckles white. The plane shuddered violently, and everything around him seemed to blur. The roar of the storm outside was matched by the terror inside the cabin. Time seemed to stretch, each second an eternity of fear and uncertainty.

Without warning, a blinding flash of light enveloped the plane, and Georgiy felt a strange sensation, as if he were being pulled in every direction at once. His vision blurred, and the sounds around him became distant echoes. The sensation intensified, and then, just as suddenly as it began, everything went black.

GEORGIY SERGEYEVICH GARBUZ

Georgiy's consciousness faded, swallowed by the void. The last thing he remembered was the chaos, the fear, and the overwhelming sense of being torn from reality. The darkness consumed him, and he was left with a profound sense of disorientation and uncertainty

Chapter 8

Georgiy's senses slowly returned, the blackness giving way to a soft, pulsating light. He felt weightless, as if suspended in a dream. The air was thick with an eerie stillness, a stark contrast to the violent turbulence moments before.

He opened his eyes and found himself bathed in a strange, ethereal glow. The cabin was silent, the passengers frozen in various states of alarm and confusion. Georgiy's breath caught in his throat as he realized they were surrounded by an otherworldly vortex—a swirling mass of light and color that seemed to stretch infinitely in all directions.

"What in the world..." he whispered, barely audible over the hum that filled the cabin.

Dr. Patel, seated beside him, slowly turned his head, his eyes wide with shock. "Georgiy, what is happening?"

"I don't know, Raj," Georgiy replied, his voice trembling. "I've never seen anything like this."

GEORGIY SERGEYEVICH GARBUZ

The vortex outside the windows twisted and writhed, its colors shifting from deep blues and purples to vibrant greens and yellows. It was mesmerizing, yet profoundly unsettling. The plane seemed to be caught in the center of this anomaly, held in a suspension that defied all known physics.

Georgiy unbuckled his seatbelt and stood up, gripping the back of his seat for support. "We need to find the captain," he said, turning to Dr. Patel and Dr. Yang. "There has to be some explanation for this."

As he made his way down the aisle, he noticed that some passengers were beginning to stir, their expressions mirroring his own confusion and fear. The vortex continued to pulse and shift, casting surreal shadows throughout the cabin.

Reaching the cockpit door, Georgiy knocked urgently. "Captain, it's Georgiy Garbuz. We need to know what's going on!"

The door opened slowly, revealing the pale faces of the captain and co-pilot. "Dr. Garbuz," the captain said, his voice strained. "We have no idea what this is. All our instruments are going haywire. We're completely disoriented."

Georgiy stepped into the cockpit, his eyes scanning the array of malfunctioning displays. The instruments flickered and beeped erratically, the readouts showing impossible data. "Is there any way to communicate with the ground?" he asked, though he already suspected the answer.

The co-pilot shook his head. "All communications are down. We tried everything. We're completely cut off."

Georgiy felt a wave of helplessness wash over him. This was beyond anything he had ever encountered, a phenomenon that defied explanation. He turned to look out the cockpit window, the swirling vortex filling his view. "Whatever this is, we need to stay calm and figure it out together," he said, trying to steady his voice.

As he returned to his seat, Georgiy noticed that the vortex seemed to be changing, its intensity increasing. The colors became more vibrant, the patterns more complex. It was as if the phenomenon was reaching some kind of climax.

Dr. Yang grabbed his arm as he sat down. "Georgiy, do you feel that?"

Before he could respond, the entire plane shuddered violently, the vortex outside accelerating its chaotic dance. A high-pitched whine filled the cabin, growing louder and more intense by the second. Georgiy felt a pressure building in his chest, the air thickening around him.

"Everyone, hold on!" he shouted, gripping his armrests.

The light intensified, blindingly bright. Georgiy shut his eyes against the searing glow, his mind racing with fear and confusion. The whine reached a deafening pitch, and then, in a split second, everything went silent.

When Georgiy opened his eyes, the vortex was gone. The plane was back in clear skies, the turbulence and the strange phenomenon vanished as suddenly as they had appeared. The cabin was eerily quiet, the passengers slowly coming to grips with what had just happened.

Georgiy looked around, his heart pounding. "Is everyone alright?" he called out.

There were nods and murmurs of assent, but the confusion and fear were still palpable. Georgiy turned to Dr. Patel and Dr. Yang, their faces reflecting the same mixture of relief and bewilderment he felt.

"What the hell was that?" Dr. Patel asked, his voice shaky.

"I don't know," Georgiy replied. "But whatever it was, it was unlike anything we've ever encountered."

As the plane continued on its path, the captain's voice came over the intercom, sounding more composed. "Ladies and gentlemen, it appears we have passed through the worst of the turbulence. We will continue our journey as planned. Please remain seated and keep your seatbelts fastened."

Georgiy leaned back in his seat, his mind racing. Whatever they had just experienced, it was clear that their journey had taken an unexpected turn. The questions about the vortex and its implications would have to wait until they reached their destination. For now, they had to focus on getting there safely.

Chapter 9

When Georgiy awoke, he felt a strange sensation of disorientation. The familiar sounds of the plane were gone, replaced by the distant hum of an unfamiliar city. He opened his eyes and found himself lying on a cold, metallic surface. His head throbbed, and his vision was blurry. As he sat up, he realized he was no longer on the plane.

He was in the middle of a bustling city, surrounded by towering skyscrapers that gleamed with advanced technology. The air was crisp and clean, and the sky above was a vibrant blue. Georgiy blinked, trying to make sense of his surroundings. The chaotic end of his flight felt like a distant nightmare, replaced by the stark reality of a future he had only dreamed of.

He stood up, feeling unsteady on his feet. The people around him were dressed in sleek, futuristic attire, their clothes made from shimmering materials that seemed to change color with the light. Vehicles glided silently along magnetic tracks, their smooth surfaces reflecting the light from the towering buildings above.

Georgiy took a deep breath, trying to calm his racing heart. The contrast between his own attire—a suit appropriate for a 2024 conference—and the avant-garde fashion of the city's inhabitants drew puzzled looks from passersby. He felt a wave of disorientation. How had he ended up here? What had caused this abrupt leap through time?

As he wandered through the city, Georgiy's thoughts raced. He needed answers, but more immediately, he needed to find someone who could help him understand this strange new world. Holographic advertisements floated in the air, displaying vibrant images of new technologies, interstellar destinations, and lifestyle products. The holograms were so lifelike that Georgiy reached out to touch one, only to have his hand pass through it.

The streets were bustling with activity, yet everything was so orderly and efficient. There were no honking cars or crowded sidewalks, just a harmonious flow of people and vehicles. The cityscape was a blend of nature and technology, with lush green spaces interspersed among the towering skyscrapers.

Georgiy approached a kiosk with a holographic interface and tentatively touched the screen. It responded instantly, presenting him with a menu of information about the city. He selected "current date," and the display flashed: May 3, 2101.

His heart skipped a beat. He had somehow traveled through time—seventy-seven years into the future. The realization hit him like a tidal wave, and he stumbled back, his mind struggling to process the implications. How was this possible? What had caused the time jump?

TIME JUMP

Georgiy continued to explore, marveling at the technological advancements and the seamless integration of sustainable practices. The city was everything he had envisioned for the future, yet it felt overwhelming to experience it firsthand. He needed to understand how he had ended up here and what this new world held for him.

As he wandered the streets, Georgiy felt a mix of awe and trepidation. The future he had dreamed of was now his reality, and he was determined to make the most of it. But first, he needed to find someone who could help him navigate this strange new world.

Chapter 10

Georgiy walked through the bustling streets of the futuristic city, his mind racing with a mixture of confusion and awe. The towering skyscrapers, their sleek designs shimmering in the sunlight, were interspersed with lush green spaces and parks, creating a harmonious blend of nature and technology. People moved about with purpose, their attire reflecting a level of sophistication and innovation he had only imagined.

He approached a nearby park, where children played with robotic pets and adults relaxed on benches that seemed to adjust to their comfort. Georgiy watched as a drone hovered overhead, delivering a package to a waiting recipient. The efficiency and tranquility of the city were both fascinating and overwhelming.

As he continued to explore, Georgiy noticed a series of holographic billboards displaying advertisements for advanced technologies—flying cars, health implants, and virtual reality experiences that seemed indistinguishable from real life. One advertisement caught his eye: a promotional video for a space colony on Mars, showcasing the thriving communities that had settled there. It was a vision of the future he had worked so hard to bring to life, now realized in ways he could scarcely believe.

Georgiy's steps led him to a bustling marketplace, where vendors sold an array of futuristic goods. He marveled at the variety of items on display—clothing made from adaptive materials, food that was nutritionally optimized, and gadgets that performed tasks he hadn't even considered. The air was filled with the hum of activity and the soft buzz of conversations in languages he recognized and others that were completely new to him.

His stomach growled, reminding him that he hadn't eaten since before the flight. He approached a food stall, where a holographic menu displayed an array of unfamiliar yet enticing dishes. The vendor, noticing his hesitation, greeted him with a warm smile.

"Good day! What can I get for you?" the vendor asked, his accent slightly different from what Georgiy was used to.

Georgiy glanced at the menu, trying to make sense of the options. "I'll have... whatever you recommend."

The vendor nodded enthusiastically. "Coming right up! You'll love our nutrient-rich smoothie and a synth-burger. Both are packed with everything you need for a healthy meal."

As he waited for his food, Georgiy took a moment to observe the people around him. They seemed happy, content, and at ease in this advanced society. It was a stark contrast to the concerns and challenges of 2024. The future, it appeared, had managed to solve many of the problems that had plagued his own time.

When the vendor handed him his meal, Georgiy thanked him and found a nearby bench to sit on. He took a tentative sip of the smoothie, surprised by its delicious taste and invigorating effect. The synth-burger, too, was a pleasant surprise—flavorful and satisfying, yet unlike anything he had tasted before.

As he ate, Georgiy's mind continued to race. He needed to understand how he had arrived in this future world and what had happened to the plane and his fellow passengers. The answers were out there, somewhere in this vast city, and he was determined to find them.

After finishing his meal, Georgiy resumed his exploration. He wandered through a residential district, where buildings seemed to grow organically from the ground, their designs seamlessly blending with the surrounding greenery. He passed a school where children were engaged in interactive lessons with holographic teachers, their eager faces reflecting the joy of learning.

Georgiy's thoughts drifted to his own work and the impact it might have had on this future. Had his research and innovations contributed to this advanced society? He felt a deep sense of pride, tempered by the urgent need to understand his new reality.

As the sun began to set, casting a golden glow over the city, Georgiy found himself at the edge of a large plaza. In the center stood a statue that caught his breath—it was a statue of himself, Georgiy Sergeyevich Garbuz. The likeness was uncanny, and the plaque at the base read:

TIME JUMP

Georgiy Sergeyevich Garbuz
Visionary Scientist and Pioneer
May 3, 1983 -

The inscription brought a lump to his throat. He had indeed played a significant role in shaping this future, but the question of how he had arrived here remained unanswered. He stood there for a long moment, lost in thought, before turning away with renewed determination.

The night was falling, and the city lights began to twinkle, casting a magical glow over the urban landscape. Georgiy knew he needed to find a place to rest and gather his thoughts. As he walked towards a nearby hotel, he couldn't shake the feeling that his journey was only just beginning. The answers he sought were out there, waiting to be discovered.

Chapter 11

Georgiy awoke the next morning feeling slightly more grounded but still overwhelmed by the events of the previous day. Determined to find answers, he set out into the city once more, his mind racing with possibilities.

As he walked through a bustling plaza, he couldn't help but marvel at the seamless blend of nature and technology that defined this future world. People moved gracefully around him, their sleek clothing and confident demeanor a testament to the advancements that had been made. He felt out of place in his outdated suit, drawing curious glances from passersby.

Unbeknownst to Georgiy, he had caught the attention of a young woman standing by a fountain in the center of the plaza. Jennifer, a striking figure with sandy blonde hair and piercing blue eyes, observed him with a mixture of curiosity and suspicion. Her attire was both elegant and practical, designed for someone accustomed to navigating the complexities of this advanced society.

She watched as Georgiy approached a kiosk with a holographic interface, fumbling slightly as he tried to make sense of the futuristic technology. There was something distinctly anachronistic about him, and it piqued her interest. With determined steps, she made her way over to him.

"Excuse me," Jennifer said, her voice clear and authoritative. "You seem a bit lost. Can I help you with something?"

Georgiy turned to face her, momentarily taken aback by her commanding presence. "I—yes, actually. I'm trying to understand where I am and what year it is."

Jennifer raised an eyebrow. "You don't know what year it is?"

Georgiy shook his head. "No, I... I believe I've traveled through time. The last thing I remember was being on a plane in 2024, and now I find myself here."

Her eyes narrowed slightly, her skepticism evident. "You expect me to believe that you've time-traveled from 2024?"

"I know it sounds unbelievable," Georgiy replied, his voice tinged with desperation. "But it's the truth. My name is Georgiy Garbuz, and I was on a flight when something extraordinary happened."

Jennifer studied him for a moment, weighing his words. There was something in his eyes—an earnestness that made her pause. "Alright, Georgiy. Let's assume for a moment that you're telling the truth. Do you have any identification on you?"

Georgiy nodded and fished his wallet out of his pocket, handing her his ID. Jennifer examined it closely, noting the outdated design and the birthdate that aligned with his story. She looked back at him, her expression softening slightly.

"Okay, Georgiy," she said, handing back his ID. "I'm Jennifer. We need to verify your story and understand the circumstances of your arrival. Come with me."

Georgiy felt a mixture of relief and anxiety. "Thank you, Jennifer. I appreciate your help."

Jennifer nodded, her demeanor a mix of professionalism and curiosity. "Follow me. We need to take you to the authorities. They'll be able to verify your story and help you figure out what happened."

As they walked through the city, Georgiy couldn't help but feel an immediate attraction to Jennifer. Her confidence and striking appearance captivated him, and despite the confusion and fear he felt, he found himself drawn to her. She moved with a grace and determination that made it hard to look away.

Jennifer led Georgiy to a sleek, modern building that seemed to blend seamlessly with its surroundings. Inside, the atmosphere was sterile and efficient, with people moving purposefully through the halls. Jennifer guided him to a small room where two officers awaited, their expressions unreadable.

"This is Georgiy Garbuz," Jennifer said, addressing the officers. "He claims to be a scientist from 2024. We need to verify his identity and his story."

One of the officers, a tall man with a stern expression, gestured for Georgiy to sit. "Please take a seat, Mr. Garbuz. We'll need to ask you a few questions."

Georgiy sat down, his heart pounding. The officers began their interrogation, scrutinizing his outdated identification documents with disbelief. They noted his birthdate of May 3, 1983—a stark contrast to the current year of 2101. Georgiy, increasingly apprehensive under the scrutiny of these futuristic authorities, struggled to comprehend the gravity of his situation.

Chapter 12

Georgiy sat in the small, sterile room, his nerves on edge as Jennifer and the two officers scrutinized his identification. The tension in the air was palpable, and Georgiy knew that this interrogation was crucial to establishing his credibility in this bewildering new world.

Jennifer took a seat across from him, her piercing blue eyes fixed on his. "Alright, Georgiy. Let's start from the beginning. You said you were on a plane in 2024. Tell us everything that happened leading up to your arrival here."

Georgiy took a deep breath, gathering his thoughts. "I was on a flight to an international scientific conference. We encountered severe turbulence, and then... then there was this vortex. It was like nothing I've ever seen before. The plane was surrounded by swirling lights and colors, and everything went black. When I woke up, I was here."

The officers exchanged glances, their skepticism evident. Jennifer leaned forward, her expression serious. "This vortex—can you describe it in more detail? What did it look like, and how did it feel?"

Georgiy nodded, trying to recall the specifics. "It was a swirling mass of light and color, shifting between blues, purples, greens, and yellows. It felt like we were suspended in the air, weightless. There was a high-pitched whine, and the air felt thick, almost oppressive. Then, everything went silent, and I woke up in your city."

Jennifer made a few notes on her tablet, her gaze never leaving Georgiy's face. "And you have no idea how you ended up here, in the year 2101?"

"None," Georgiy replied. "One moment, I was on the plane, and the next, I was here. I can't explain it."

The officers murmured among themselves, their voices low. Jennifer looked at Georgiy with a mixture of curiosity and concern. "Your story is hard to believe, Georgiy, but your identification checks out. It's outdated, but it's authentic. We need to verify your identity and conduct some tests to understand what happened."

Georgiy nodded, feeling a small measure of relief. "Thank you. I just want to understand how I got here and if there's any way to return to my own time."

Jennifer stood up, signaling the end of the initial interrogation. "We'll do everything we can to help you, Georgiy. For now, please cooperate with the authorities. They will take you to a secure location where we can run some tests and gather more information."

As the officers led him out of the room, Georgiy couldn't help but feel a growing connection to Jennifer. She had been skeptical at first, but her demeanor had softened as he explained his situation. He appreciated her professionalism and her willingness to help him despite the outlandish nature of his story.

The walk through the futuristic building was a blur. Georgiy's mind raced with questions and concerns. He needed to understand the science behind his time travel, if it was indeed possible, and what had caused it. More importantly, he needed to find a way back to his own time.

Arriving at another secure room, Georgiy was asked to sit while the officers prepared the necessary equipment for their tests. He glanced around, taking in the advanced technology and the sterile, efficient environment. It was both fascinating and intimidating.

Jennifer entered the room, her expression focused and determined. "Georgiy, we'll start with some basic tests to establish your physical and genetic profile. This will help us confirm your identity and rule out any potential anomalies."

Georgiy nodded, submitting himself to the procedures. As the officers conducted their tests, Jennifer observed closely, occasionally making notes on her tablet. The process was thorough and meticulous, leaving no room for doubt or error.

As the tests concluded, Jennifer turned to Georgiy with a thoughtful expression. "It will take some time to analyze the results, but we're making progress. In the meantime, you'll be placed in a secure room where you can rest. If you need anything, don't hesitate to ask."

"Thank you, Jennifer," Georgiy said, his voice sincere. "I appreciate everything you're doing."

Jennifer gave him a small, reassuring smile. "We're all curious about how you ended up here, Georgiy. Rest assured, we'll do our best to help you find the answers you need."

Chapter 13

The sterile, secure room where Georgiy had undergone his initial interrogation felt like a holding cell, though the officers and Jennifer treated him with respect and courtesy. After the tests were completed, the officers escorted him to another area of the building, while Jennifer walked alongside him, a thoughtful expression on her face.

They entered an elevator, and Jennifer pressed a button for a lower floor. As the doors closed, Georgiy glanced at her, feeling a mix of gratitude and curiosity. "Jennifer, I appreciate your help. This whole situation is overwhelming, and I don't know what I would have done without your guidance."

Jennifer gave him a small smile. "It's my job to help, Georgiy. Your story is unique, and if it's true, it could have significant implications. We're all eager to understand what happened and how we can assist you."

The elevator descended smoothly, and Georgiy felt a slight pressure in his ears as they went deeper underground. When the doors opened, they stepped into a high-security area filled with advanced technology and bustling personnel. The atmosphere was tense but focused, with people moving purposefully from one task to another.

Jennifer led him through a series of corridors until they reached a large room with a long table and several chairs. The walls were lined with screens displaying various data streams and holographic images. At the head of the table stood a distinguished-looking man and woman, both dressed in the sleek, futuristic uniforms that seemed standard in this time.

"Dr. Garbuz, this is Prime Minister Chen and President Reed," Jennifer introduced, her tone respectful. "They are the leaders of our International Intergalactic Space Federation or the IISF. They have been briefed on your situation and are here to discuss the next steps."

Georgiy's eyes widened in shock. The IISF was his creation, an idea he had tirelessly advocated for during his lifetime. He had envisioned an international organization dedicated to space exploration and colonization, but to see it realized was beyond his wildest dreams.

Prime Minister Chen, a woman with sharp features and a commanding presence, noticed his reaction and smiled slightly. "I see you're familiar with the IISF. It appears your vision has had a lasting impact, Dr. Garbuz."

Georgiy felt a mix of pride and disbelief. He approached the table and extended his hand. "Prime Minister Chen, President Reed, it's an honor to meet you. Thank you for taking the time to see me."

Prime Minister Chen shook his hand firmly. "Dr. Garbuz, your arrival is indeed unusual. We are here to ensure that we fully understand your situation and provide the assistance you need."

President Reed, a tall man with a calm demeanor and piercing eyes, nodded in agreement. "Please, have a seat. We have many questions, and I'm sure you do as well."

Georgiy sat down, feeling the weight of their scrutiny. Jennifer took a seat beside him, ready to support and facilitate the conversation. Prime Minister Chen began by summarizing the information they had gathered so far, including the results of the preliminary tests.

"Dr. Garbuz, your identification and genetic profile confirm that you are indeed from the year 2024," Chen stated. "This presents a unique challenge, as we have no record of time travel being possible. Can you elaborate further on the events that led to your arrival here?"

Georgiy recounted his experience once more, detailing the strange vortex, the blinding light, and the disorienting transition from the plane to the futuristic city. He spoke carefully, aware of the extraordinary nature of his story and the skepticism it might provoke.

As he finished, President Reed leaned forward, his expression thoughtful. "If what you describe is accurate, this could have significant implications for our understanding of space-time and quantum mechanics. We need to conduct more in-depth tests to analyze the exact nature of this phenomenon."

Prime Minister Chen nodded in agreement. "We will provide you with all necessary resources and support, Dr. Garbuz. Your cooperation is crucial in uncovering the truth behind your time travel. In the meantime, you will be granted access to our facilities and given accommodations here at the IISF."

Jennifer turned to Georgiy, her expression reassuring. "We'll ensure you have everything you need, Georgiy. This is a secure environment, and we'll be working closely with you to understand and potentially reverse the process that brought you here."

Georgiy felt a mixture of relief and determination. He was in capable hands, and though the path ahead was uncertain, he was not alone. "Thank you, Prime Minister Chen, President Reed, and Jennifer. I'm committed to cooperating fully and finding answers to this extraordinary situation."

Prime Minister Chen stood, signaling the end of the meeting. "We'll reconvene once we have more information from the additional tests. Jennifer will escort you to your accommodations and ensure you're settled in. Welcome to the future, Dr. Garbuz."

As Georgiy followed Jennifer out of the room, he couldn't help but feel a renewed sense of purpose. The future was a place of incredible potential, and he was determined to make the most of this unexpected journey.

Chapter 14

After the meeting with Prime Minister Chen and President Reed, Jennifer led Georgiy through a series of corridors to another secure room. This one was smaller and more intimate, designed for detailed interrogations and discussions. The room was equipped with advanced technology, including holographic displays and recording devices.

Jennifer gestured for Georgiy to take a seat at the central table. "Please, sit down, Georgiy. The officials will be here shortly to conduct a more thorough interrogation. I will stay with you to assist."

Georgiy nodded and sat down, trying to steady his nerves. The room's sterile environment reminded him of the many laboratories he had worked in during his career, but the stakes here felt much higher. He was about to be questioned not only about his identity but also about the extraordinary phenomenon that had brought him to this future.

Moments later, the door opened, and two officials entered. One was a tall man with a serious demeanor, and the other a woman with a sharp gaze that seemed to miss nothing. They introduced themselves as Agent Collins and Dr. Lang, specialists in temporal anomalies and quantum physics.

"Dr. Garbuz," Agent Collins began, taking a seat across from him, "we've reviewed the initial information provided by Jennifer and conducted some preliminary tests. Your situation is unique, and we need to understand it fully. Let's start with the basics. Can you describe in detail the events leading up to your arrival here?"

Georgiy recounted his story once more, providing as much detail as he could remember. He described the vortex, the swirling lights, the disorienting sensations, and the sudden transition from the plane to the futuristic city. As he spoke, Dr. Lang made notes on a holographic tablet, occasionally asking for clarification on specific points.

"These phenomena you describe," Dr. Lang interjected, "they align with some theoretical models we've developed for quantum disturbances and temporal shifts. However, we've never observed such an event in practice. Your account suggests a highly localized and intense disturbance."

Agent Collins leaned forward, his expression serious. "Dr. Garbuz, we need to know if there were any other anomalies or unusual occurrences leading up to the flight. Anything at all, no matter how insignificant it might seem."

Georgiy thought carefully. "There was nothing out of the ordinary before the flight. The turbulence started suddenly, and then the vortex appeared. It was unlike anything I've ever encountered in my research."

Dr. Lang nodded thoughtfully. "We'll need to conduct more detailed analyses of your physical and neurological state to understand any potential effects of the temporal shift. This will include brain scans, genetic profiling, and other advanced diagnostics."

Georgiy felt a mix of anxiety and determination. "I'll cooperate fully. I want to understand what happened just as much as you do."

The interrogation continued, with the officials probing every aspect of Georgiy's experience and his understanding of temporal mechanics. They asked about his research background, his theories on space-time, and his vision for the International Intergalactic Space Federation.

As the questioning progressed, Georgiy couldn't help but notice Jennifer's supportive presence. She occasionally offered clarifications or insights that seemed to guide the officials' inquiries in productive directions. Her knowledge of the futuristic world and her understanding of Georgiy's predicament were invaluable.

After what felt like hours, the officials concluded their interrogation. Agent Collins stood, his expression more relaxed. "Thank you for your cooperation, Dr. Garbuz. We'll analyze the data we've gathered and keep you informed of our findings. For now, you can return to your accommodations."

Dr. Lang added, "We'll need to conduct further tests tomorrow. Please be prepared for a comprehensive series of examinations."

Georgiy nodded, feeling both exhausted and relieved. "Thank you. I'll be ready."

Jennifer stood and gestured for Georgiy to follow her. As they walked back to his accommodations, she gave him an encouraging smile. "You did well, Georgiy. The officials are thorough, but they're also committed to finding the truth. We'll get to the bottom of this."

Georgiy felt a surge of gratitude. "Thank you, Jennifer. Your support means a lot to me. I don't know what I would do without you."

She smiled warmly. "We're in this together, Georgiy. Now, get some rest. Tomorrow will be another long day, but we'll face it one step at a time."

As Georgiy settled into his room, he couldn't help but reflect on the day's events. The future was a place of incredible promise and potential, but it also held many mysteries. With Jennifer's help and the resources of the IISF, he was determined to uncover the truth behind his extraordinary journey.

Chapter 15

The following morning, Georgiy woke up in his futuristic accommodations feeling a mix of apprehension and determination. The previous day's interrogation had left him with more questions than answers, but he was resolved to uncover the truth. After a quick breakfast of nutrient-rich food, which tasted surprisingly good, he was ready to face the day.

Jennifer arrived promptly, her presence a comforting constant in this disorienting new world. "Good morning, Georgiy. Are you ready for another round of tests and questions?"

Georgiy nodded, trying to muster a smile. "As ready as I'll ever be. Let's get to it."

Jennifer led him through the maze-like corridors of the IISF facility, finally arriving at a high-tech lab filled with advanced diagnostic equipment. Dr. Lang and several other scientists were already there, preparing for the day's tests.

"Good morning, Dr. Garbuz," Dr. Lang greeted him with a nod. "We'll start with some advanced neurological scans to better understand any potential impacts of the temporal shift."

The tests were thorough and intricate, involving a series of scans and examinations that left Georgiy feeling like a lab specimen. Throughout the process, Jennifer remained by his side, providing explanations and reassurance.

After what felt like hours, the tests finally concluded. Dr. Lang approached Georgiy, her expression serious but tinged with curiosity. "We've gathered a significant amount of data, Dr. Garbuz. The preliminary results are fascinating, but we need more time to analyze everything fully."

Jennifer stepped forward, her eyes meeting Georgiy's. "While they work on the analysis, I think it's time we had a more in-depth conversation. There's something important you need to know."

Curiosity piqued, Georgiy followed Jennifer to a quiet, private office. She gestured for him to sit, then took a seat across from him. The room was filled with holographic displays and interactive surfaces, a testament to the advanced technology of this era.

"Georgiy," Jennifer began, her tone gentle but firm, "you've mentioned the year 2024 several times. The truth is, we're currently in the year 2101. You've traveled through time—seventy-seven years into the future."

Georgiy's heart skipped a beat. Hearing it confirmed so plainly was overwhelming. "2101," he repeated, trying to wrap his mind around the implications. "That's... incredible. How is this even possible?"

Jennifer took a deep breath. "Time travel, as far as we know, has never been achieved intentionally. What happened to you is unprecedented. The vortex you described might be a rare temporal anomaly—something that disturbed the fabric of space-time and transported you here."

Georgiy sat back, processing the information. "I can't believe it. All my life, I dreamed of advancing humanity's understanding of space and time, but to actually experience this... it's beyond anything I imagined."

Jennifer smiled softly. "Your contributions to science were indeed significant, Georgiy. The International Intergalactic Space Federation, or IISF, was founded based on your visionary ideas. You inspired generations of scientists and explorers, and your legacy continues to shape our future."

The weight of her words sank in, filling Georgiy with a profound sense of pride and responsibility. "I never thought my ideas would have such a lasting impact. It's humbling."

Jennifer nodded. "Your work laid the foundation for many of the advancements you see today. And now, you have the opportunity to learn from this future and perhaps even contribute to it in ways you never expected."

Georgiy felt a surge of determination. "I want to understand every-thing—how I got here, what caused the anomaly, and how I can possibly return to my own time."

Jennifer's expression turned serious. "That's our goal as well. The IISF will provide you with all the resources and support you need. Together, we'll uncover the truth behind your journey through time."

Georgiy looked at her, feeling a deep connection and gratitude. "Thank you, Jennifer. Your support means everything to me."

She smiled warmly. "We're in this together, Georgiy. Now, let's get back to the lab and see what we can discover."

As they returned to the high-tech lab, Georgiy felt a renewed sense of purpose. The future was a place of incredible potential, and with Jennifer and the IISF by his side, he was determined to make the most of this unexpected journey. The path ahead was uncertain, but Georgiy was ready to face whatever challenges lay in store.

Chapter 16

Georgiy woke up the next morning with a renewed sense of purpose. The previous day's revelations had left him feeling both overwhelmed and inspired, but he was determined to adapt to this new world and contribute to it in any way he could. Jennifer arrived at his quarters promptly, her presence a reassuring constant in this disorienting future.

"Good morning, Georgiy," she greeted him with a warm smile. "Today, we'll be getting you outfitted with attire and equipment suitable for our environment. Follow me."

Georgiy followed Jennifer through the sleek, futuristic corridors of the IISF facility. The walls were lined with displays showcasing the organization's history and achievements, a testament to the incredible advancements that had been made since his time. They arrived at a spacious room filled with advanced clothing and equipment. The walls were lined with shelves holding various items, from adaptive clothing to high-tech gadgets. A friendly technician greeted them.

"Dr. Garbuz, welcome," the technician said, extending a hand. "I'm Alex, and I'll be helping you get outfitted today. Let's start with the basics—clothing."

Alex guided Georgiy to a section of the room where a variety of clothing items were displayed. "In this era, our clothing is designed to be adaptive and multifunctional. The fabrics adjust to temperature changes, provide optimal comfort, and even have built-in health monitoring features."

Georgiy marveled at the selection. The clothing ranged from formal wear to casual and athletic attire, each piece looking sleek and modern. The colors were vibrant, and the materials had a subtle sheen that hinted at their advanced nature. Alex handed him a set of clothes that looked both stylish and comfortable. "Try these on," Alex suggested.

Georgiy changed into the new attire and was amazed at how it felt against his skin. The fabric was soft and flexible, adjusting perfectly to his movements. It felt cool initially but warmed up to a comfortable temperature as he moved. "This is incredible," he remarked. "It feels like a second skin."

Jennifer smiled. "Our advancements in material science have allowed us to create clothing that enhances both comfort and functionality. You'll find it much more suitable for our environment."

Next, Alex showed Georgiy a variety of gadgets and equipment. "This is a personal assistant device," Alex explained, handing Georgiy a small, sleek gadget. "It will help you navigate our world, access information, and communicate with others. It integrates seamlessly with our holographic interfaces."

Georgiy examined the device, intrigued by its capabilities. Alex demonstrated how it projected holographic displays and responded to voice commands. "You can use this device to access maps, send messages, and even control various aspects of your environment," Alex explained. "It's designed to be intuitive and user-friendly."

The device felt surprisingly light in Georgiy's hand, and he marveled at its sleek design. Alex continued to explain its features, demonstrating how it could connect to the building's network, display real-time data, and even translate languages. "This will be essential for you as you acclimate to our society," Alex said.

After getting outfitted with the necessary clothing and equipment, Georgiy felt more prepared to face this new world. The adaptive clothing felt like a protective layer, and the personal assistant device gave him a sense of connection to his surroundings. Jennifer and Alex guided him back to the main facility, where Jennifer had arranged a tour of the IISF.

As they walked, Jennifer explained more about the advancements that had been made in clothing and personal technology. "Our clothing not only adjusts to environmental conditions but also monitors your health. Sensors embedded in the fabric can track your vital signs, detect stress levels, and even administer basic medical care if needed."

Georgiy was impressed. "This level of integration and functionality is beyond anything we had in my time. It's like wearing a personal health and comfort assistant."

Jennifer nodded. "Exactly. Our goal has always been to enhance the quality of life through technology. The personal assistant device you're carrying is another example of that. It provides seamless access to information and services, making everyday tasks more manageable and efficient."

Chapter 17

T hey arrived at a large atrium filled with holographic displays showcasing various projects and achievements. Jennifer introduced Georgiy to several key figures, including Dr. Li, the head of astrophysics, and Dr. Fernandez, the chief engineer.

"Dr. Garbuz, it's an honor to meet you," Dr. Li said, shaking Georgiy's hand. "Your work laid the foundation for much of what we do here. We're eager to hear your insights and collaborate on new projects."

Georgiy felt a sense of pride and responsibility. "Thank you, Dr. Li. I'm looking forward to learning more about your work and contributing in any way I can."

Jennifer continued the tour, showing Georgiy the state-of-the-art laboratories, where scientists were conducting experiments on advanced propulsion systems, quantum mechanics, and bioengineering. The level of innovation and collaboration was astounding, and Georgiy felt both inspired and humbled by the achievements of this future society.

They passed through a section dedicated to robotics. "This is where we develop our robotic systems," Jennifer explained. "We've made significant advancements in creating robots that can assist with everything from medical procedures to space exploration."

Georgiy observed a demonstration where a humanoid robot performed complex tasks with precision and efficiency. The robot moved with a fluidity and dexterity that was almost human-like, seamlessly executing intricate operations. It assembled delicate components with speed and accuracy, demonstrating the technological prowess of this era.

"Our robots are designed to handle a variety of tasks," Jennifer continued. "In the medical field, they can assist surgeons in performing delicate procedures with greater precision. In space exploration, they can withstand harsh environments and perform tasks that would be too dangerous for humans."

Georgiy was fascinated by the level of sophistication and versatility of the robots. "The integration of robotics into daily life and specialized fields has clearly transformed how we operate."

Jennifer nodded. "Indeed. Robots have become indispensable partners in our efforts to explore new frontiers and improve the quality of life. They've also helped us achieve efficiencies and capabilities that were unimaginable in your time."

The tour concluded with a visit to the command center, a vast room filled with holographic screens displaying real-time data from various space missions. Engineers and scientists monitored the progress of exploratory vessels, space stations, and planetary colonies.

"This is the nerve center of our operations," Jennifer said. "From here, we coordinate our missions and ensure the safety and success of our endeavors."

Georgiy was in awe of the scale and sophistication of the IISF's operations. The realization that his ideas had helped shape this remarkable future filled him with a renewed sense of purpose.

As they exited the command center, Jennifer turned to Georgiy with a smile. "There's still so much more to show you, but for now, let's take a break. You've had a lot to absorb."

Georgiy appreciated the respite. "Thank you, Jennifer. This has been incredible. I'm eager to learn more and see how I can contribute."

Jennifer led him to a comfortable lounge area, where they could relax and reflect on the tour. As they sat down, Georgiy felt a deep sense of connection to this future world and the people working to make it better. He knew that his journey was just beginning, and he was ready to embrace the challenges and opportunities that lay ahead.

Chapter 18

After a short break, Jennifer and Georgiy continued their discussion in the lounge area. The advanced and comfortable surroundings offered a stark contrast to the environments Georgiy was used to, further underscoring the advancements of this future world.

"Now that you've seen some of the facilities," Jennifer began, "let's delve into the broader technological and societal advancements that have shaped our society since your time."

Georgiy leaned forward, eager to learn more. "I'm fascinated by what I've seen so far. Please, tell me more."

Jennifer smiled and activated a holographic display that projected images and data around them. "One of the most significant changes has been in the field of energy. We've developed advanced fusion reactors that provide clean, virtually limitless power. This breakthrough has eliminated our reliance on fossil fuels and drastically reduced our carbon footprint."

The display showed a model of a fusion reactor, its complex design shimmering in the air. Jennifer explained how these reactors worked, using magnetic confinement to sustain fusion reactions and generate immense amounts of energy. "These reactors have transformed our energy infrastructure, enabling us to power cities, industries, and space missions with unparalleled efficiency."

Georgiy was captivated by the details. "It's incredible. This would have been a game-changer in my time. What about transportation?"

Jennifer nodded and the display shifted to show various modes of transportation. "Transportation has also seen revolutionary advancements. We've perfected magnetic levitation and propulsion systems. Our vehicles, both terrestrial and extraterrestrial, are faster, more efficient, and environmentally friendly."

She showed Georgiy a holographic model of a sleek, futuristic car gliding silently along a magnetic track. "This technology has revolutionized how we travel, reducing commute times and minimizing our impact on the environment."

Georgiy marveled at the progress. "It's amazing to see how far we've come. And what about healthcare?"

Jennifer smiled, clearly proud of the advancements in this area. "Healthcare has also undergone a profound transformation. We've developed nanotechnology for medical purposes, allowing us to treat diseases at the cellular level. Our diagnostic tools are incredibly precise, and our treatments are highly effective."

She described how nanobots could be used to repair damaged tissues, target cancer cells, and even enhance the body's natural healing processes. "These advancements have extended our lifespans and improved our quality of life significantly."

Georgiy listened intently, absorbing the information. "This level of medical technology would have seemed like science fiction in my time. It's wonderful to see how it's benefiting people."

Jennifer continued, "In terms of communication, we've made significant strides as well. Holographic technology has transformed how we interact, making remote communication as immersive as in-person meetings. This has not only improved personal communication but also enhanced global collaboration."

The display shifted to show people engaging in holographic meetings, their lifelike projections interacting seamlessly. "Education has also benefited from these advancements," Jennifer added. "With interactive learning environments, education has become more personalized and accessible."

Georgiy was particularly interested in this aspect. "Education has always been a key to progress. How have these changes impacted society as a whole?"

Jennifer's expression grew thoughtful. "Our society has made great strides in addressing social issues. We've implemented universal basic income and comprehensive social safety nets, reducing poverty and inequality. Our focus on sustainability and community has created a more harmonious and inclusive world."

Georgiy felt a deep sense of awe and gratitude. "This future is everything I hoped for and more. It's a testament to what humanity can achieve when we work together."

Jennifer nodded. "Your vision and dedication played a crucial role in making this possible. And now, you have the chance to be a part of it."

As they continued their discussion, Georgiy couldn't help but feel inspired by the advancements and the potential they represented. The future was not only technologically advanced but also more equitable and sustainable. It was a vision realized, one that he had long dreamed of and worked towards.

Their conversation was interrupted by a soft chime, indicating that it was time for their next appointment. Jennifer looked at Georgiy with a smile. "It's time to visit our space exploration division. You'll get to see firsthand the achievements we've made in planetary colonization."

Georgiy's excitement grew. "I've been looking forward to this. Let's go."

Jennifer led him through the corridors once more, their destination the division dedicated to humanity's ventures beyond Earth. As they walked, Georgiy felt a renewed sense of purpose and determination. The advancements he had seen were just the beginning, and he was eager to learn more and contribute to this incredible future.

Chapter 19

Jennifer led Georgiy through the sleek corridors of the IISF headquarters, their destination the space exploration division dedicated to humanity's ventures beyond Earth. The walls were adorned with murals and holographic displays depicting various milestones in space colonization, from the first steps on Mars to the establishment of lunar bases.

As they entered a large briefing room, Georgiy's eyes widened at the sight of detailed models of celestial bodies and advanced spacecraft. Engineers and scientists moved about, busy with their work, but they paused to acknowledge Jennifer and Georgiy with respectful nods.

"Dr. Garbuz, welcome," Dr. Fernandez, the chief engineer, greeted him warmly. "We're excited to share our achievements in space colonization with you."

The presentation began with a holographic model of Mars, the red planet rotating slowly in the air above the table. "Mars was our first major success," Dr. Fernandez explained. "We established self-sustaining colonies with advanced habitats that support human life. These habitats are equipped with life support systems, agricultural modules, and recreational facilities."

Georgiy watched in amazement as the holographic display showcased thriving Martian colonies, complete with bustling communities and lush greenhouses. The habitats were domed structures, designed to withstand the harsh Martian environment while providing a comfortable living space for the inhabitants. "We've also terraformed parts of the planet, making it more hospitable for long-term habitation."

Dr. Fernandez continued, "Beyond Mars, we've established research outposts and mining operations on several moons and asteroids. These outposts are crucial for resource extraction and scientific exploration."

The display shifted to show colonies on the moons of Jupiter and Saturn. "Our efforts have expanded to include Europa, Titan, and other moons. Each location presents unique challenges, but our technology and expertise have allowed us to overcome them."

Georgiy was particularly fascinated by the advancements in propulsion technology that enabled these missions. "We've developed advanced propulsion systems that significantly reduce travel time between planets," Dr. Fernandez explained. "These systems use a combination of nuclear fusion and ion propulsion, making interplanetary travel more feasible and efficient."

The presentation then moved to the lunar colonies. "The Moon serves as a vital hub for our space exploration efforts," Dr. Fernandez said. "Its proximity to Earth makes it an ideal location for launching missions deeper into space. We've established multiple bases on the lunar surface, equipped with laboratories, residential areas, and even recreational facilities."

The holographic display showed bustling lunar bases, with scientists conducting experiments, engineers working on spacecraft, and families enjoying the low-gravity environment. "The Moon has become a thriving community and a stepping stone for our further exploration efforts," Dr. Fernandez added.

Georgiy felt a profound sense of accomplishment and excitement. "This is truly remarkable. The potential for human expansion and exploration is limitless."

Jennifer smiled, sharing in his enthusiasm. "And it's all thanks to visionaries like you, Georgiy. Your work laid the groundwork for these achievements, and now you can be a part of the next phase of our journey."

Dr. Fernandez highlighted the next frontier in space exploration—exoplanets. "Our next goal is to establish colonies on exoplanets within neighboring star systems," he said. "We're currently developing the technology needed for faster-than-light travel and long-duration space missions."

The display shifted to show distant star systems and potential exoplanetary targets. "These missions will be challenging, but the rewards are immense," Dr. Fernandez continued. "Expanding humanity's reach beyond our solar system will open up new opportunities for scientific discovery and human settlement."

Georgiy felt a surge of pride and determination. The advancements he had seen were a testament to human ingenuity and perseverance. "This future is everything I hoped for and more," he said. "I'm eager to contribute to these efforts and help shape the next chapter of our exploration."

As the presentation concluded, Dr. Fernandez and his team answered Georgiy's questions, providing detailed insights into the technical and logistical aspects of space colonization. Georgiy was particularly interested in the collaborative efforts between different nations and organizations, which had played a crucial role in these achievements.

Jennifer led Georgiy out of the briefing room, her eyes shining with excitement. "There's still so much more to show you, but I hope this gives you a sense of the incredible advancements we've made."

Georgiy nodded, feeling both humbled and inspired. "It's amazing to see how far we've come. The future is bright, and I'm honored to be a part of it."

As they walked back towards the main facility, Georgiy couldn't help but feel a deep connection to this future world. The challenges and opportunities that lay ahead were immense, but with the support and collaboration of brilliant minds, he was confident that humanity's potential was limitless.

Chapter 20

After the awe-inspiring presentation on space colonization, Jennifer led Georgiy to a quieter section of the IISF headquarters. They arrived at a scenic rooftop garden, an oasis of greenery with a panoramic view of the futuristic city below. The garden was designed for relaxation and reflection, offering a peaceful respite from the high-tech surroundings.

Jennifer gestured to a bench under a blooming tree. "I thought we could take a moment here. It's a favorite spot of mine."

Georgiy nodded, appreciating the serene atmosphere. They sat down, and for a moment, they simply enjoyed the tranquil setting. The cityscape stretched out before them, a testament to human ingenuity and progress.

"Jennifer," Georgiy began, breaking the silence, "I've seen so much today, and it's been incredible. But I'd like to know more about you. How did you come to work here at the IISF?"

Jennifer smiled, a hint of pride in her expression. "I grew up fascinated by space and technology. My parents were both scientists, and they instilled in me a love for exploration and discovery. Joining the IISF was a natural choice for me. It's a place where I can contribute to humanity's future and be part of something greater than myself."

Georgiy listened intently, feeling a growing connection to her. "It's clear that you're passionate about your work. Your dedication is inspiring."

Jennifer's smile widened. "Thank you, Georgiy. I've always believed that the pursuit of knowledge and the betterment of humanity are the most important goals we can strive for. Working here allows me to do that every day."

They sat in companionable silence for a few moments, the gentle rustle of leaves providing a soothing backdrop. Georgiy felt a sense of peace he hadn't experienced since his arrival in this future world.

"Tell me about your work," Jennifer said, turning the conversation back to Georgiy. "What inspired you to pursue a career in science?"

Georgiy leaned back, his mind drifting to memories of his early years. "I was born in Esik, a small town in the Almaty Region of Kazakhstan, back when it was part of the former USSR. My childhood was shaped by the stark contrasts of that era—scientific progress on one hand, and political oppression on the other. My parents were teachers, and they nurtured my curiosity about the world. We didn't have much, but they always encouraged me to dream big."

Jennifer listened with rapt attention. "It sounds like your upbringing had a profound impact on you."

Georgiy nodded. "It did. Growing up in Esik, I was always fascinated by the stars. On clear nights, I'd lie on the grass and gaze up at the vast expanse of the sky, wondering what lay beyond. My father told me stories about cosmonauts and the space race, and those tales fueled my imagination. Despite the hardships, I found hope and inspiration in the possibilities of space exploration."

He paused, lost in thought for a moment. "When the Soviet Union collapsed, my family faced new challenges. We decided to immigrate to the USA, seeking better opportunities. The transition wasn't easy, but it opened up new worlds for me. I immersed myself in my studies, driven by a desire to understand the universe and contribute to humanity's progress."

Jennifer's eyes sparkled with admiration. "Your journey is incredible, Georgiy. The determination and resilience you've shown are remarkable."

Georgiy smiled, appreciating her kind words. "Thank you, Jennifer. The move to the USA was transformative. It allowed me to access advanced education and connect with like-minded individuals who shared my passion for science. I pursued my studies in physics and engineering, always with an eye toward the stars."

He continued, "My work on space-time theories and propulsion systems was driven by a belief that humanity's future lies beyond Earth. I wanted to develop technologies that would make interstellar travel possible, opening up new frontiers for exploration and discovery. It's humbling to see that some of my ideas have contributed to the advancements of this era."

Jennifer placed a reassuring hand on his arm. "Your contributions have had a lasting impact, Georgiy. Your vision and dedication played a crucial role in shaping the future we live in today."

Georgiy felt a mix of pride and humility. "It's incredible to see how far we've come. But I have to admit, being here, in this future, it's overwhelming. There's so much to learn, so much to understand."

Jennifer's touch was comforting. "You don't have to do it alone, Georgiy. We're here to help you. The IISF is built on collaboration and shared knowledge. Together, we'll continue to explore and discover new frontiers."

Georgiy looked at Jennifer, grateful for her support. "Thank you, Jennifer. Your kindness and understanding mean a lot to me. I feel like I'm beginning to find my place here."

Jennifer's eyes softened. "I'm glad to hear that, Georgiy. You're not just a visitor from the past; you're a valuable part of our future."

As the sun began to set, casting a golden glow over the city, they continued to talk, sharing stories of their lives, their dreams, and their hopes for the future. The bond between them grew stronger with each passing moment, built on mutual respect and a shared passion for discovery.

The rooftop garden was bathed in the warm hues of twilight, and the first stars began to twinkle in the sky. Georgiy felt a sense of contentment and anticipation. He was ready to face whatever challenges lay ahead, knowing that he had allies and friends in this new world.

"Jennifer," Georgiy said, breaking the comfortable silence, "I want to be more than just an observer here. I want to contribute, to be a part of this incredible journey. Where do you think I can make the most impact?"

Jennifer considered his question thoughtfully. "Your expertise in space-time theories and propulsion systems is invaluable. We have ongoing projects that could benefit greatly from your insights. And given your unique perspective, you might see solutions we've overlooked."

Georgiy nodded, feeling a renewed sense of purpose. "I'd like that. I'm eager to get started."

Jennifer smiled, her eyes shining with enthusiasm. "I'll make the arrangements. Tomorrow, we'll begin integrating you into our research teams. There's so much potential for collaboration and innovation."

As they stood to leave, Georgiy felt a surge of optimism. The future was a place of boundless possibilities, and with Jennifer and the IISF by his side, he was ready to embrace it fully.

Together, they walked back into the heart of the IISF headquarters, ready to embark on the next phase of their journey, united by a shared vision of progress and exploration.

Chapter 21

The next morning, Jennifer escorted Georgiy to the central research facility within the IISF headquarters. The building was a marvel of modern architecture, with sleek lines and expansive glass walls that allowed natural light to flood the interior. As they walked through the bustling corridors, Jennifer filled Georgiy in on what to expect.

"You're going to meet some of the brightest minds in our field," she said, her eyes sparkling with excitement. "They've been eagerly anticipating your arrival."

Georgiy nodded, feeling a mixture of anticipation and nervousness. He had always thrived in collaborative environments, but this was different. These were scientists from a future he was only beginning to understand.

They arrived at a large conference room where a group of researchers was already gathered. The room was filled with holographic displays showing complex equations, simulations of space-time distortions, and models of advanced propulsion systems. The air buzzed with intellectual energy.

Jennifer led Georgiy to the front of the room and introduced him. "Everyone, this is Dr. Georgiy Garbuz. As you know, he's the pioneering scientist whose work laid the foundation for many of our current advancements."

The researchers greeted him with a warm round of applause, and Georgiy felt a surge of pride and responsibility. He stepped forward, addressing the group. "Thank you, everyone. It's an honor to be here. I'm excited to learn about your work and contribute in any way I can."

Dr. Li, the head of astrophysics, stepped forward. He was a tall man with sharp features and an air of authority. "Dr. Garbuz, welcome. We've been looking forward to your insights. Let me introduce you to the team."

Dr. Li introduced the key members of the research team: Dr. Amara Patel, a brilliant theoretical physicist; Dr. Lucas Fernandez, an expert in advanced propulsion systems; and Dr. Sofia Moreno, a specialist in quantum mechanics. Each scientist greeted Georgiy warmly, and he could sense their genuine enthusiasm.

Dr. Patel led the way to a large table covered with holographic schematics and data streams. "We're currently working on refining our understanding of space-time distortions and how to harness them for faster-than-light travel," she explained. "Your work on space-time theories has been instrumental in getting us this far."

Georgiy leaned over the table, examining the data. "These models are impressive. What are the main challenges you're facing?"

Dr. Fernandez chimed in. "One of the biggest issues is stabilizing the space-time distortions to create a sustainable warp field. We've made progress, but we're encountering unexpected energy fluctuations that disrupt the field."

Georgiy nodded thoughtfully. "It sounds like the energy fluctuations might be related to quantum entanglement effects. Have you considered using entangled particles to stabilize the field?"

Dr. Moreno's eyes lit up. "That's an intriguing idea. We've been exploring different stabilization methods, but incorporating entangled particles could provide the additional control we need."

The team dove into a deep discussion, exploring the potential of Georgiy's suggestion. He felt invigorated by the exchange of ideas, his mind racing with possibilities. It was clear that this team was not only highly skilled but also open to innovative approaches.

As the hours passed, Georgiy became more familiar with the team's ongoing projects. He offered his insights on various aspects of their research, from theoretical models to practical applications. The collaborative atmosphere reminded him of his early days in scientific research, filled with the excitement of discovery and the thrill of pushing boundaries.

Jennifer watched from the sidelines, a proud smile on her face. She could see that Georgiy was already making a significant impact. As the day drew to a close, she approached him. "You've made quite an impression, Georgiy. The team is excited about the new directions your ideas have opened up."

Georgiy smiled, feeling a sense of accomplishment. "It's been an incredible day. I'm grateful for the opportunity to work with such brilliant minds."

Jennifer nodded. "This is just the beginning. Tomorrow, we'll continue exploring your ideas and how they can integrate with our projects. For now, let's get some rest."

As they walked back to his quarters, Georgiy reflected on the day's events. He felt a renewed sense of purpose and was eager to continue contributing to this remarkable future. The challenges were immense, but with the support of his new colleagues and the resources of the IISF, he was confident that they could achieve great things.

Chapter 22

The following days were a whirlwind of activity for Georgiy as he immersed himself in the work of the IISF research team. Each morning, he joined the team in the central research facility, eager to collaborate and share his insights. The team quickly adapted to his presence, valuing his unique perspective and experience.

Dr. Patel and Dr. Fernandez were particularly interested in Georgiy's ideas on stabilizing space-time distortions. They spent hours discussing the theoretical underpinnings and practical applications of his suggestions. The team worked tirelessly, running simulations and refining their models to incorporate Georgiy's concepts.

One morning, as they gathered around a large holographic display, Dr. Moreno presented the latest simulation results. "We've made significant progress in stabilizing the warp field using entangled particles. The energy fluctuations have decreased by 40%, but we're still encountering some instability at higher power levels."

Georgiy studied the data, his mind racing with possibilities. "What if we adjust the phase alignment of the entangled particles? It could help synchronize the energy distribution and further reduce the fluctuations."

Dr. Fernandez nodded thoughtfully. "That's a great idea. Let's run a simulation with the adjusted parameters and see how it affects the stability."

As they worked, Georgiy found himself forming strong bonds with his new colleagues. Their shared passion for discovery and innovation created a camaraderie that transcended the boundaries of time. He admired their dedication and brilliance, and they respected his deep knowledge and creative thinking.

During breaks, they shared stories and experiences, further strengthening their connections. Dr. Patel recounted her early days as a physicist, inspired by the pioneering work of scientists like Georgiy. Dr. Fernandez spoke of his fascination with space travel and the thrill of working on cutting-edge propulsion systems.

One afternoon, while taking a break in the facility's atrium, Dr. Moreno approached Georgiy with a thoughtful expression. "Georgiy, I've been thinking about your journey to our time. It must be overwhelming to see how much has changed."

Georgiy smiled, appreciating her concern. "It is overwhelming, but it's also exhilarating. Seeing the advancements and knowing that my work contributed to this future is incredibly rewarding. And having supportive colleagues like all of you makes it easier to adapt."

Dr. Moreno nodded. "We're grateful to have you with us. Your insights have already made a significant impact, and I'm sure we'll achieve even greater things together."

The atmosphere was charged with excitement and a sense of purpose. Georgiy felt reinvigorated, his passion for discovery reignited by the collaborative spirit of the team.

One evening, after a particularly productive day, Jennifer invited Georgiy to join her for dinner in the rooftop garden. The setting sun cast a golden glow over the city, creating a serene and romantic atmosphere.

"Georgiy, you've been doing incredible work," Jennifer said as they sat down at a small table set with a simple but elegant meal. "How are you feeling about everything?"

Georgiy took a moment to reflect. "I feel energized and inspired. Collaborating with the team has been a rewarding experience. It's amazing to see how our combined efforts are pushing the boundaries of what's possible."

Jennifer smiled warmly. "I'm glad to hear that. Your contributions have been invaluable, and the team really appreciates your presence."

As they enjoyed their meal, the conversation turned more personal. Jennifer leaned in, curiosity gleaming in her eyes. "What drives you, Georgiy? You've achieved so much, and yet you continue to push the boundaries. What keeps you motivated?"

Georgiy paused, contemplating his answer. "I've always believed that humanity's greatest strength is its ability to dream and to strive for those dreams, no matter how impossible they may seem. My motivation comes from a deep desire to see humanity thrive and reach its full potential. But above all, I'm driven by the hope of inspiring the next generation—especially kids. They are the future, and I want to give them the tools and opportunities to achieve what might seem impossible today."

Jennifer listened intently, her admiration growing. "That's an inspiring perspective. It's clear that your passion has driven you to accomplish incredible things."

Georgiy nodded. "Passion is essential, but so is perseverance. There were many times when the obstacles seemed insurmountable, but giving up was never an option. I've always felt a responsibility to contribute to the greater good, to use my knowledge and skills to help solve the challenges we face. When I see children learning and dreaming about the stars, it reinforces my commitment. They remind me of why I started this journey in the first place."

Jennifer's smile was tender. "I feel the same way, Georgiy. It's one of the reasons I'm so dedicated to my work. Seeing the impact of our efforts, knowing that we're making a difference, it makes all the hard work worthwhile."

Georgiy looked into her eyes, feeling a deep connection. "You've been a wonderful guide and support, Jennifer. I've come to value our time together immensely. Your encouragement has been crucial in helping me navigate this new world."

Jennifer's eyes softened. "I'm glad to hear that. You've brought a new perspective and energy to our work. And I've enjoyed getting to know you on a personal level as well."

The evening ended with a sense of warmth and mutual understanding. Georgiy felt a growing affection for Jennifer, and he sensed that she felt the same. Their bond, forged through shared passion and respect, was blossoming into something more.

As they walked back to his quarters, Georgiy felt a renewed sense of purpose and belonging. He was not only making a significant impact on the future but also building meaningful relationships that enriched his life in ways he hadn't anticipated.

The following morning, the team convened to discuss the latest developments. As they reviewed the data, Dr. Li received an urgent message. His expression grew serious as he read it.

"Everyone, I've just received word from our temporal mechanics division," Dr. Li announced. "They've been analyzing the temporal anomaly that brought Georgiy here, and they've discovered something important."

A silence fell over the room as the implications of this revelation sank in. Georgiy felt a mixture of emotions—relief at the prospect of understanding his situation, but also a hint of apprehension. He had grown attached to this future and the people in it.

Dr. Li continued, his tone cautious. "They believe the anomaly is inherently unstable. While we don't know exactly when, it's likely that

Georgiy's presence here is temporary. We need to make the most of our time and ensure his contributions are fully integrated into our work."

Jennifer looked at Georgiy with concern. "We'll focus on finalizing our current projects and documenting your insights thoroughly. Let's make the most of the time we have."

Georgiy nodded, determined to make every moment count. "Agreed. Let's get to work."

Chapter 23

The next day, Jennifer met Georgiy at the entrance of the IISF headquarters, a look of excitement on her face. "I have something special planned for today," she said, her eyes sparkling. "We're going to visit the Garbuz Space School Academies."

Georgiy's heart swelled with pride and curiosity. "I've heard about them, but seeing them in person will be incredible. Lead the way."

They boarded a sleek, futuristic vehicle that glided silently along the streets, powered by the advanced propulsion systems Georgiy had helped conceptualize. The cityscape passed by in a blur of towering structures and lush greenery, a testament to the harmonious blend of technology and nature that defined this future world.

As they approached the academy, Georgiy was struck by its grand design. The campus sprawled across several acres, with buildings that combined cutting-edge architecture with sustainable practices. Solar panels glistened in the sunlight, and vertical gardens adorned the walls, providing both aesthetic beauty and environmental benefits.

Jennifer guided Georgiy through the main entrance, where they were greeted by a holographic display showcasing the history and achievements of the Garbuz Space School Academies. Students of various ages bustled around, their faces alight with enthusiasm and curiosity.

"The academy was founded in your honor, Georgiy," Jennifer explained as they walked through the halls. "It's dedicated to nurturing the next generation of scientists, engineers, and explorers. Your work has inspired countless young minds."

Georgiy felt a deep sense of fulfillment as he watched the students engage in animated discussions and hands-on projects. "This is everything I dreamed of and more. Seeing these kids so passionate about learning and discovery is truly heartening."

Jennifer led him to a large auditorium where a class was in session. The room was equipped with advanced teaching tools, including holographic projectors and interactive displays. The students were immersed in a lesson on space-time theory, guided by a dynamic young teacher.

As they entered, the teacher looked up and smiled. "Ah, Dr. Garbuz, what an honor to have you here. Students, I'd like you to meet the man whose groundbreaking work laid the foundation for much of what we study today."

The students' eyes widened with awe and excitement. Georgiy felt a wave of humility and pride as he addressed them. "Thank you for the warm welcome. It's wonderful to see such bright young minds eager to explore the wonders of science. Remember, the future is yours to shape. Dream big, work hard, and never stop asking questions."

One student raised her hand. "Dr. Garbuz, what inspired you to become a scientist?"

Georgiy smiled, recalling his earlier conversation with Jennifer. "I've always believed in the power of dreams and perseverance. But what truly drives me is the hope of inspiring the next generation—students like you. I want to give you the tools and opportunities to achieve what might seem impossible today."

The students listened intently, their eyes shining with inspiration. After the class, Georgiy spent time interacting with the students, answering their questions and encouraging their aspirations. He was deeply moved by their enthusiasm and the realization that his work had touched so many lives.

As they toured the rest of the academy, Jennifer pointed out various facilities, including state-of-the-art laboratories, workshops, and a planetarium. "The academy is designed to provide a comprehensive education, blending theoretical knowledge with practical experience," she explained. "We want our students to be well-rounded and ready to tackle the challenges of the future."

Georgiy nodded, impressed by the thoughtful design and dedication to excellence. "It's clear that a lot of care and effort has gone into creating this environment. The students here are fortunate to have such incredible resources and support."

The tour concluded with a visit to the academy's Innovation Center, where students were working on independent projects and research. Georgiy was particularly impressed by a group of young engineers developing a new propulsion system. Their innovative approach and creative problem-solving reminded him of his early days in research.

Jennifer smiled as she watched Georgiy interact with the students. "You can see the impact of your legacy here, Georgiy. These kids are the future, and they're building on the foundation you helped create."

Georgiy felt a deep sense of gratitude and purpose. "This is the greatest reward I could ask for. Knowing that my work has inspired and will continue to inspire future generations is more than I ever dreamed of."

As they left the academy, Georgiy couldn't help but feel a renewed sense of motivation. The visit had reminded him of the importance of nurturing young minds and the profound impact that education and inspiration could have on the world.

"Thank you, Jennifer," Georgiy said, turning to her with a grateful smile. "This visit was exactly what I needed. It's given me a renewed sense of purpose."

Jennifer nodded, her eyes filled with warmth. "I'm glad to hear that, Georgiy. Your legacy lives on in these students, and together, we'll continue to push the boundaries of what's possible."

With a sense of determination and optimism, Georgiy returned to the IISF headquarters, ready to tackle the challenges ahead and contribute

to the bright future he had seen at the Garbuz Space School Academies.

Chapter 24

Back at the IISF headquarters, Georgiy and the research team resumed their work with renewed vigor. The visit to the Garbuz Space School Academies had not only inspired Georgiy but had also reaffirmed the importance of their mission.

Dr. Li called for a meeting in the central research facility to discuss their progress and address the ongoing challenges they faced. The room was filled with holographic displays showing complex equations, simulations, and models of their latest propulsion systems.

"Everyone, we've made significant progress in stabilizing the warp field using entangled particles," Dr. Li began. "However, we're still encountering instability at higher power levels. We need to find a solution to maintain stability across all power ranges."

Georgiy studied the data on the holographic displays, his mind racing with possibilities. "We've adjusted the phase alignment of the entangled particles, but perhaps we need to consider a dynamic approach that adapts in real-time to the energy fluctuations."

Dr. Patel looked intrigued. "A self-adjusting mechanism within the warp field generator could constantly fine-tune the phase alignment based on real-time feedback. It would be complex but might provide the stability we need."

Dr. Fernandez nodded. "It's worth exploring. We can start by developing a prototype and running simulations to test the concept."

The team divided into smaller groups, each focusing on different aspects of the proposed solution. Georgiy worked closely with Dr. Patel and Dr. Fernandez to design the self-adjusting mechanism. They spent hours brainstorming, sketching out designs, and coding algorithms for the prototype.

After several intense days of work, the team gathered to test the prototype. The atmosphere was charged with anticipation as they initiated the simulation. The holographic display showed the warp field stabilizing and adapting in real-time to the energy fluctuations.

"It's working!" Dr. Moreno exclaimed, her face lighting up with excitement. "The dynamic adjustments are maintaining stability even at higher power levels."

Georgiy felt a surge of satisfaction. "This is a significant breakthrough. With further refinement, we can achieve a stable and sustainable warp field."

As they celebrated their success, an alert sounded from the central control system. Dr. Li's expression turned serious as he read the incoming data. "We have an unexpected consequence. The dynamic adjustments are creating a feedback loop that's affecting the surrounding space-time fabric. We need to address this before it causes any disruptions."

The room fell silent as the team processed the new challenge. Georgiy stepped forward, his mind already formulating a plan. "We need to create a damping mechanism to absorb the excess energy from the feedback loop. It should prevent the disturbances from propagating and destabilizing the space-time fabric."

Dr. Patel nodded in agreement. "We can integrate the damping mechanism into the existing design. It will require precise calibration, but it's achievable."

The team set to work, combining their expertise to develop the damping mechanism. They ran multiple simulations, each iteration bringing them closer to a solution. The process was arduous, but their determination never wavered.

Finally, after several more days of relentless effort, the team was ready to test the updated prototype. The tension in the room was palpable as they initiated the simulation. The holographic display showed the warp field stabilizing, the dynamic adjustments in action, and the damping mechanism effectively absorbing the excess energy.

"It's stable," Dr. Fernandez said, his voice filled with relief and triumph. "We've managed to achieve a sustainable warp field without causing any disruptions."

Georgiy felt a profound sense of accomplishment. "This breakthrough opens up new possibilities for space travel and exploration. It's a testament to our collaborative efforts and dedication."

As the team celebrated their success, Dr. Li approached Georgiy with a thoughtful expression. "Georgiy, your unique perspective and insights have been invaluable in achieving this breakthrough. We couldn't have done it without you."

Georgiy smiled, feeling a deep sense of belonging. "Thank you, Dr. Li. It's been an honor to work with such a talented and dedicated team."

Jennifer, who had been observing the entire process, joined them. "Congratulations, everyone. This is a significant milestone. Georgiy, your contributions have made a lasting impact."

Georgiy looked at Jennifer, his heart swelling with gratitude and affection. "I'm grateful for the opportunity to be part of this journey. Together, we've achieved something extraordinary."

The celebration continued, but Georgiy couldn't shake a lingering feeling of uncertainty. The revelation from the temporal mechanics division still weighed on his mind. He knew that his time in the future might be limited, and he was determined to make every moment count.

As the evening drew to a close, Georgiy and Jennifer found a quiet corner to talk. "Jennifer, there's something I've been thinking about. Our work here is important, but so is the legacy we leave for future

generations. The visit to the Garbuz Space School Academies reminded me of that."

Jennifer nodded, her eyes reflecting his sentiment. "You're right,
Georgiy. Inspiring and nurturing young minds is crucial. We need to
ensure that our breakthroughs and knowledge are passed on to them."

Georgiy took her hand, feeling a deep connection. "Let's make that
our mission. No matter what happens, we'll ensure that the future is
in good hands."

Jennifer smiled, squeezing his hand gently. "I'm with you, Georgiy.
Together, we'll build a legacy that will inspire generations to come."

With a renewed sense of purpose and determination, Georgiy and
Jennifer rejoined the team, ready to continue their work and make the
most of their time together.

Chapter 25

After their breakthrough with the warp field stability, the team decided to take a well-deserved break. Georgiy and Jennifer found themselves once again in the rooftop garden, a favorite spot where they could escape the bustling activity of the IISF headquarters. The evening was warm and serene, with the city lights twinkling below them.

As they sat on a bench under a blooming tree, Jennifer turned to Georgiy with a thoughtful expression. "Georgiy, you've been here for a while now, and I can see how much you've contributed. But I've been wondering, how do you feel about everything that's happened? About being here, knowing it's temporary?"

Georgiy sighed, gazing out at the horizon. "It's been an incredible journey, Jennifer. Seeing the advancements, meeting the team, and contributing to these groundbreaking projects—it's more than I ever imagined. But the uncertainty of my time here weighs on me. I know I could be transported back to my own time at any moment."

Jennifer placed a comforting hand on his arm. "I can't imagine how difficult that must be. But you've made such a difference, Georgiy. Your work here will continue to inspire and drive us forward, even if you do return to the past."

Georgiy turned to her, his eyes reflecting a mixture of gratitude and affection. "Thank you, Jennifer. Your support has been invaluable. I've grown to care deeply about this future and the people in it. And I've come to care deeply about you."

Jennifer's eyes softened, and she smiled tenderly. "I feel the same way, Georgiy. Our time together has been special. I've admired your dedication and passion, and I've enjoyed every moment we've spent together."

Georgiy reached out and took her hand, his heart pounding. "Jennifer, I don't know how much time we have left, but I want to make the most of it. You've become so important to me, and I don't want to waste any more time."

Jennifer squeezed his hand gently, her gaze locking with his. "Then let's not. Let's make every moment count, starting now."

They leaned in, and their lips met in a tender, passionate kiss. It felt as if the world around them melted away, leaving only the two of them, connected by their shared experiences and deepening affection. When they finally pulled apart, Georgiy cupped Jennifer's face in his hands, his eyes searching hers.

"I don't know what the future holds," he said softly, "but I want to spend every possible moment with you, Jennifer."

Jennifer smiled, her eyes glistening with emotion. "And I want the same, Georgiy. We'll face whatever comes together."

They spent the rest of the evening talking, sharing their dreams and fears, and growing even closer. The bond between them strengthened, fueled by their mutual respect and the urgency brought on by the uncertainty of Georgiy's presence in this future.

Later that night, as they walked back to Georgiy's quarters, Jennifer spoke about the upcoming mission assigned by the IISF. "Tomorrow, we'll be briefed on a critical new mission. It's based on our recent breakthroughs, and it's something that could have a significant impact on our future research."

Georgiy nodded, feeling a renewed sense of purpose. "I'm ready for it. Let's make the most of whatever time we have."

Jennifer smiled, her grip on his hand tightening. "Together, we can achieve anything."

They arrived at Georgiy's quarters, and Jennifer hesitated for a moment before speaking. "Georgiy, I want you to know that no matter what happens, you've changed my life. You've made me believe that anything is possible."

Georgiy leaned in and kissed her gently. "And you've changed mine, Jennifer. You've given me hope and a reason to keep fighting. Whatever happens, I'll always be grateful for our time together."

With one last embrace, Jennifer left Georgiy's quarters, and he watched her go, feeling a mix of happiness and apprehension. He knew that their time together might be limited, but he was determined to make every moment count.

As he lay in bed that night, Georgiy reflected on his journey, his achievements, and the people who had become so important to him. He felt a deep sense of fulfillment, knowing that he had made a difference. But he also felt a pang of sadness, knowing that his time in this future might be drawing to a close.

The next day would bring new challenges and opportunities, and Georgiy was ready to face them with Jennifer by his side. Together, they would continue to push the boundaries of what was possible, fueled by their love and their shared vision for a better future.

Chapter 26

The following morning, Georgiy arrived at the IISF briefing room, feeling a mixture of anticipation and determination. Jennifer was already there, along with Dr. Li, Dr. Patel, Dr. Fernandez, and Dr. Moreno. The room was filled with a palpable sense of excitement, and Georgiy could see that everyone was eager to get started.

Dr. Li began the briefing, his tone confident and authoritative. "Thank you all for being here. As you know, our recent breakthroughs in stabilizing the warp field have opened up new possibilities for our research and exploration. Today, we're going to discuss a critical new mission that will build on these advancements."

He activated a holographic display, showing a detailed schematic of a new spacecraft. "This is the Aurora, our latest exploration vessel equipped with the stabilized warp field generator. Our mission is to test the generator's capabilities in deep space and gather data on its performance under various conditions."

Georgiy leaned forward, studying the schematic with keen interest. The Aurora was a marvel of engineering, designed to push the boundaries of human exploration. He felt a surge of pride knowing that his contributions had played a role in its development.

Dr. Patel took over, explaining the mission objectives. "We'll be conducting a series of experiments to measure the warp field's stability, efficiency, and impact on the surrounding space-time fabric. Our goal is to ensure that the generator can sustain long-duration missions and support future colonization efforts."

Dr. Fernandez added, "We'll also be testing the Aurora's new propulsion systems, which combine nuclear fusion and ion propulsion for maximum efficiency. This mission will provide invaluable data to refine these technologies and pave the way for interstellar travel."

As the briefing continued, Georgiy couldn't help but feel a sense of urgency. The scientists were still researching the temporal anomaly that had brought him to this future, and there was always the possibility that he could be transported back to his own time at any moment. He knew that every contribution he made now could have a lasting impact.

After the briefing, Jennifer approached Georgiy with a smile. "Excited about the mission?"

Georgiy nodded. "Absolutely. This is an incredible opportunity. I'm looking forward to seeing how the warp field generator performs in real-world conditions."

Jennifer's eyes sparkled with enthusiasm. "And it's all happening because of your work, Georgiy. You've made such a difference."

Georgiy felt a deep sense of gratitude. "Thank you, Jennifer. I couldn't have done it without the support of you and the team."

They spent the rest of the day preparing for the mission, working closely with the team to finalize the plans and ensure that everything was ready. Georgiy marveled at the level of coordination and expertise that went into every aspect of the mission. It was clear that the IISF was a well-oiled machine, driven by a shared passion for exploration and discovery.

As they worked, Georgiy and Jennifer stole moments to be together, their bond growing stronger with each passing hour. The uncertainty of Georgiy's time in the future added a layer of intensity to their relationship, making every interaction more meaningful.

That evening, after a long day of preparations, Georgiy and Jennifer found themselves alone in one of the quieter corners of the facility. The atmosphere was charged with emotion, and Georgiy could see the concern in Jennifer's eyes.

"Jennifer," he began, taking her hands in his, "I don't know how much time I have left here, but I want you to know how much you mean to me. You've made my time in this future so much more than I ever imagined."

Jennifer's eyes filled with tears, but she smiled bravely. "Georgiy, you've changed my life too. I've never felt this way about anyone before. No matter what happens, I'll always cherish our time together."

They embraced, holding each other tightly as if trying to make the moment last forever. The uncertainty of the future hung over them, but they found solace in their connection.

The next morning, the team gathered at the launch site, where the Aurora stood ready for its maiden voyage. The sleek vessel gleamed in the morning light, a symbol of human ingenuity and the relentless pursuit of knowledge.

Dr. Li addressed the team, his voice filled with pride and determination. "Today, we embark on a journey that will push the boundaries of our understanding and pave the way for future generations. Let's make history."

Georgiy and the team boarded the Aurora, each member taking their positions and preparing for launch. The atmosphere was electric, filled with anticipation and excitement.

As the countdown began, Georgiy glanced at Jennifer, who gave him a reassuring smile. He felt a surge of confidence, knowing that he was part of something truly extraordinary.

The engines roared to life, and the Aurora lifted off, ascending into the sky with a powerful grace. Georgiy watched as the Earth fell away beneath them, feeling a profound sense of awe and wonder.

The mission had begun, and Georgiy was ready to face whatever challenges lay ahead. With Jennifer and the team by his side, he knew they could achieve anything.

Chapter 27

T he morning after the successful launch of the Aurora, Jennifer had a new plan for the day. She met Georgiy with a look of excitement. "Today, I want to show you another aspect of your legacy," she said. "We're visiting the hospital to meet patients who are benefiting from your medical innovations."

Georgiy's interest was piqued. "I'd love that, Jennifer. Let's go."

They boarded a transport vehicle, and Jennifer navigated through the city towards the hospital. The drive was filled with pleasant conversation, their bond growing stronger with every moment.

Upon arriving at the hospital, Georgiy was impressed by the modern, yet welcoming design. The building was filled with natural light, and the air was infused with a sense of hope and healing. Jennifer led him to the main reception area, where they were greeted by Dr. Elena Rojas, the head of the hospital.

"Dr. Garbuz, it's an honor to meet you," Dr. Rojas said warmly, shaking his hand. "Your work has made a tremendous impact on our patients' lives."

"Thank you, Dr. Rojas. I'm looking forward to seeing it firsthand," Georgiy replied, feeling a mix of pride and humility.

Their first stop was the pulmonary care unit. Dr. Rojas introduced them to a young woman named Lila, who was sitting comfortably in her room, reading a book. She looked up with a smile as they entered.

"Lila, this is Dr. Georgiy Garbuz," Dr. Rojas said. "He developed the medical inhaler device and lung treatment you're using."

Lila's eyes widened with gratitude. "Dr. Garbuz, thank you so much. Your treatment has changed my life. I've had severe asthma since I was a child, and this inhaler has made it so much easier to breathe and live a normal life."

Georgiy felt a lump in his throat. "I'm so glad to hear that, Lila. Knowing that my work has helped you means everything to me."

They spent a few more minutes talking with Lila, who shared her experiences and the difference the treatment had made. Georgiy listened intently, feeling a profound sense of fulfillment.

Next, they visited the organ transplant unit. Dr. Rojas led them to a room where a middle-aged man named Marco was recovering from a recent liver transplant. The room was filled with flowers and cards from well-wishers.

"Marco, this is Dr. Georgiy Garbuz," Dr. Rojas said. "He developed the organ technology used in your transplant."

Marco's face lit up with appreciation. "Dr. Garbuz, I owe you my life. I was on the transplant waiting list for years. Your technology made it possible for me to get a new liver and a second chance at life."

Georgiy shook Marco's hand, deeply moved. "I'm honored, Marco. Your strength and resilience are truly inspiring."

As they continued their tour, Jennifer and Georgiy couldn't help but notice the subtle signs of heightened security around the hospital. Guards were stationed at key points, and the staff seemed a bit on edge. Jennifer exchanged a concerned glance with Georgiy but didn't say anything at the moment.

Their final stop was the mental health unit. Dr. Rojas introduced them to a young man named Ethan, who was engaged in an art therapy session. The walls were adorned with vibrant paintings and drawings, creating a colorful and uplifting environment.

"Ethan, this is Dr. Georgiy Garbuz," Dr. Rojas said. "He developed the art therapy program you're participating in."

Ethan looked up from his painting, a wide smile spreading across his face. "Dr. Garbuz, thank you. This program has helped me so much. I've struggled with depression for years, and art therapy has given me a way to express myself and find peace."

Georgiy felt a deep sense of connection with Ethan. "I'm glad to hear that, Ethan. Art has always been a powerful form of expression. Keep creating and sharing your gift with the world."

As they left the mental health unit, Georgiy turned to Jennifer, his heart full. "This has been an incredible experience, Jennifer. Seeing the impact of my work on these patients is beyond rewarding."

Jennifer smiled, her eyes shining with pride. "You've made a real difference, Georgiy. And there's so much more we can do together."

They walked back to the reception area, where Dr. Rojas thanked them for their visit. As they prepared to leave, Jennifer's communicator beeped with an urgent message. She glanced at it, her expression turning serious.

"Georgiy, we need to talk," she said quietly, leading him to a private corner.

"What's going on?" Georgiy asked, sensing the tension.

Jennifer lowered her voice. "There's been increased activity from a rival group within the IISF. They're not supportive of our current leadership and have their own agenda. We've received intelligence that they might be planning something. The heightened security here isn't just a precaution; it's a response to a credible threat."

Georgiy's mind raced. "Do you think they're after me?"

Jennifer nodded. "It's possible. Your presence here and the impact of your work have made you a target. We need to be cautious and stay vigilant."

As they left the hospital, Georgiy couldn't shake the feeling that they were being watched. The ride back to the IISF headquarters was tense, both of them scanning their surroundings for any signs of danger.

When they arrived, Jennifer pulled Georgiy aside. "We'll need to increase your security and keep a low profile. The team is already working on it. In the meantime, stay close and trust no one outside our circle."

Georgiy nodded, feeling a mix of fear and determination. "I'll do whatever it takes to stay safe and continue our work."

Jennifer squeezed his hand, her eyes filled with resolve. "We're in this together, Georgiy. We'll face whatever comes, side by side."

As they walked into the headquarters, Georgiy knew that their journey was far from over. The threat from the rival group was real, and they would need to be vigilant and prepared. But with Jennifer and the team by his side, he was ready to face any challenge.

Chapter 28

B ack at the IISF headquarters, the atmosphere was thick with unease. The revelation that a rival faction within the IISF was planning something sinister had everyone on edge. The security around Georgiy was tightened, and the research team was on high alert.

Jennifer and Georgiy were in the central research facility, going over the latest data from the Aurora's mission. Despite the tension, they tried to focus on their work. The discoveries made during the mission were groundbreaking, and they knew that their efforts could pave the way for the future of space exploration.

As they worked, Jennifer's communicator beeped. She glanced at it and her expression grew serious. "Georgiy, there's something we need to discuss. Let's go to a more private place."

They moved to a secure meeting room, away from prying eyes and ears. Jennifer closed the door and turned to Georgiy, her face filled with concern.

"The intelligence reports have confirmed that the rival group within the IISF is planning to abduct you," she said quietly. "Their motivations are political. They don't agree with our current leadership and believe that capturing you could give them leverage."

Georgiy felt a chill run down his spine. "Why me? What do they hope to achieve by abducting me?"

Jennifer sighed. "Your presence here is a symbol of our progress and our future. They see you as a key figure who could shift the balance of power in their favor. By taking you, they hope to undermine the current leadership and push their own agenda."

Georgiy nodded, understanding the gravity of the situation. "We need to be cautious. My stay here is temporary, but I can't let them use me as a pawn in their game."

Jennifer reached out and took his hand. "We'll protect you, Georgiy. We're working on increasing your security, but we need to be vigilant. Trust no one outside our circle."

As they left the meeting room, the tension between them and the rest of the team was palpable. They knew that they had to stay focused and united to face the impending threat.

Later that evening, Jennifer and Georgiy found a quiet moment together in the rooftop garden. The stars above them twinkled, offering a serene contrast to the turmoil they were facing.

"Jennifer," Georgiy began, breaking the silence, "I've been thinking a lot about our work and the impact it has on the future. Knowing that my time here might be limited makes every moment feel even more precious."

Jennifer nodded, her eyes reflecting the same sentiment. "I feel the same way, Georgiy. Every moment we spend together is valuable. I wish we didn't have to worry about these threats, but we'll face them together."

Georgiy took her hand, his heart swelling with affection. "No matter what happens, I want you to know how much you mean to me. You've made this journey so much more meaningful."

Jennifer smiled, leaning in to kiss him gently. "You mean the world to me, Georgiy. We'll get through this, and we'll continue to make a difference together."

Their embrace was a moment of solace amidst the growing tension. They knew that the challenges ahead would test their resolve, but their bond gave them the strength to face whatever came their way.

The following days were filled with heightened security measures and constant vigilance. The research team continued their work, but the threat of the rival faction loomed over them. Every move was calculated, every interaction scrutinized.

Georgiy and Jennifer grew closer, their relationship deepening with each passing day. The uncertainty of Georgiy's stay added an intensity to their connection, making every moment they shared even more significant.

One evening, as they reviewed the latest data from the Aurora's mission, Dr. Li entered the room, his expression grave. "We've received credible intelligence that the rival group is planning to make their move soon. We need to be prepared for anything."

Georgiy felt a surge of determination. "We won't let them disrupt our work. We need to stay focused and united."

Jennifer nodded, her resolve matching his. "We'll protect you, Georgiy. Together, we'll face whatever comes."

As the team gathered to discuss their strategy, the sense of urgency was palpable. They knew that they were up against a formidable opponent, but their shared commitment to their mission and each other gave them the strength to persevere.

The night before the anticipated attack, Georgiy and Jennifer found a moment of quiet in the rooftop garden. The stars shone brightly above them, a reminder of the vastness of the universe and the importance of their work.

"Jennifer," Georgiy said softly, taking her hand, "whatever happens, I want you to know that I'm grateful for every moment we've had together. You've given me hope and strength."

Jennifer smiled, her eyes glistening with emotion. "And you've given me a reason to believe in a better future, Georgiy. We'll face this together, no matter what."

Their kiss was a promise of unity and resilience. As they held each other under the stars, they knew that they were ready to face the challenges ahead, side by side.

Chapter 29

The following morning, the atmosphere at the IISF headquarters was tense. Dr. Li had called an emergency meeting to discuss the latest intelligence reports. Georgiy, Jennifer, and the rest of the core team gathered in the conference room, their faces reflecting the gravity of the situation.

Dr. Li stood at the head of the table, his expression serious. "We have received credible intelligence that the rival faction within the IISF is planning a major attack on our headquarters. Their goal is to abduct Dr. Garbuz and disrupt our research."

A murmur of concern swept through the room. Jennifer exchanged a worried glance with Georgiy, who felt a knot of tension in his stomach.

Dr. Patel spoke up, her voice steady but tense. "What do we know about their plans? How soon could they strike?"

Dr. Li projected a holographic map of the headquarters, highlighting potential entry points and vulnerable areas. "Our intelligence suggests that they could strike within the next 48 hours. We need to strengthen our defenses and prepare for a full-scale confrontation."

Dr. Fernandez nodded, his jaw set with determination. "We'll need to secure all entry points and increase our security presence throughout the facility. We should also set up a command center to coordinate our defense efforts."

Dr. Moreno added, "We need to ensure that our research data and equipment are protected. If they manage to breach our defenses, we can't let them access our work."

Georgiy listened intently, feeling a surge of determination. "What can I do to help?"

Dr. Li looked at him, his eyes filled with respect. "Your safety is our top priority, Dr. Garbuz. But your knowledge and expertise will be invaluable in helping us prepare. We need to ensure that the anomaly remains stable and that our research is protected."

Jennifer squeezed Georgiy's hand. "We'll get through this, Georgiy. We've faced challenges before, and we've come out stronger. This time will be no different."

The team spent the next several hours preparing for the anticipated attack. Security personnel were stationed at key points throughout the headquarters, and advanced surveillance systems were activated to monitor for any signs of an impending breach. The tension was palpable, but so was the sense of unity and determination.

Georgiy worked closely with Dr. Fernandez and Dr. Moreno to reinforce the security protocols around the temporal anomaly. They developed contingency plans to ensure that the anomaly remained stable, even in the event of an attack.

Jennifer coordinated the efforts of the security team, ensuring that everyone was on high alert and ready to respond at a moment's notice. She moved through the facility with calm authority, her presence reassuring to everyone around her.

As the day turned to night, the team gathered in the command center, ready for whatever might come. The air was thick with anticipation, and every sound seemed magnified in the tense silence.

Georgiy sat next to Jennifer, his hand resting on hers. "Whatever happens, we face it together," he said softly.

Jennifer nodded, her eyes resolute. "Together. Always."

Chapter 30

The hours passed slowly, each one filled with a sense of impending danger. The team remained vigilant, their eyes on the surveillance monitors and their ears attuned to any unusual sounds.

Suddenly, an alarm blared, and the surveillance monitors lit up with activity. Figures moved swiftly through the shadows, approaching the perimeter of the headquarters.

"They're here," Dr. Li said grimly. "Everyone, to your positions."

The team sprang into action, moving with practiced precision. Security personnel armed themselves and took up defensive positions, while the research team prepared to protect their work and ensure the stability of the anomaly.

Georgiy and Jennifer stood together in the command center, their hearts pounding with adrenaline. "Stay close," Jennifer said, her voice firm. "We'll get through this."

As the rival faction breached the outer defenses, the sounds of conflict echoed through the corridors. The battle had begun, and the stakes had never been higher. The team was ready to defend their headquarters, their research, and each other.

Georgiy stood beside Jennifer in the command center, their eyes fixed on the surveillance monitors. The rival faction moved with precision, cutting through the outer defenses with alarming efficiency.

"Sector 3 breach!" a security officer shouted, his voice tense.

"We need reinforcements there now," Jennifer commanded, her voice steady. "Dr. Fernandez, keep monitoring the anomaly. Georgiy, stay with me."

Georgiy nodded, his heart racing. He followed Jennifer as they moved through the facility, directing the security personnel and coordinating the defense.

In the corridor, they encountered a group of the faction's operatives. The intruders were equipped with advanced weaponry and moved with military precision.

"Engage!" Jennifer shouted.

In another part of the facility, Dr. Fernandez and Dr. Moreno were working frantically to maintain the stability of the anomaly. The console in front of them beeped with warnings as the rift fluctuated under the stress of the ongoing battle.

"Adjust the phase alignment!" Dr. Fernandez shouted over the alarms.

Dr. Moreno's hands flew over the controls. "I'm on it! We need to stabilize the energy levels or the whole thing could collapse!"

The ground shook with the force of nearby explosions. Dr. Fernandez glanced at the monitor, his face set with grim determination. "We can't let them take Georgiy. We have to hold it together."

Meanwhile, Georgiy and Jennifer continued to lead the defense. They moved through the facility, repelling the intruders and ensuring that their team held the critical points.

As they reached another breach point, Georgiy saw a group of operatives trying to hack into the mainframe. He aimed his weapon and fired, forcing them to retreat.

"Good shot!" Jennifer called out, covering him as they advanced.

The battle raged on, each side pushing the other to their limits. The rival faction was well-equipped and relentless, but the IISF team fought with a fierce resolve born of their commitment to their mission and loyalty to one another.

In the command center, Dr. Li coordinated the defense efforts, his voice calm but commanding. "Sector 5, we need more support there. Keep the mainframe secure at all costs."

The security personnel responded with precision, their movements coordinated and efficient. They held the line, pushing back the intruders with a combination of strategy and sheer determination.

As the battle reached its peak, Georgiy and Jennifer found themselves back at the command center. The tension was almost unbearable, but they remained focused.

"We're holding them off, but we need to secure the mainframe and the anomaly," Jennifer said, her voice strained but determined.

Georgiy nodded, his resolve unshaken. "We'll make it. We have to."

Together, they led a final push to secure the critical areas of the facility. The rival faction's operatives fought with desperate intensity, but the IISF team's unity and determination proved to be their greatest strength.

In the end, the rival faction was repelled, their forces driven back and their plans thwarted. The IISF team stood victorious, but not without cost. Several team members were injured, and the headquarters had suffered significant damage.

Georgiy and Jennifer stood together in the aftermath, their bodies weary but their spirits unbroken. They had faced the threat head-on and emerged stronger for it.

Chapter 31

The battle had been fierce, but the IISF team had managed to repel the initial wave of the rival faction's attack. However, the danger was far from over. The rival operatives regrouped outside the headquarters, preparing for a renewed assault.

Georgiy and Jennifer, along with the rest of the team, gathered in the command center to reassess their strategy. The room was filled with tension and urgency as they prepared for the next phase of the confrontation.

Dr. Li spoke with determination. "We've managed to hold them off for now, but they will be back. We need to strengthen our defenses and prepare for a coordinated counterattack."

Dr. Patel added, "Our priorities to protect Georgiy and ensure the stability of the anomaly. We can't let them breach our defenses again."

As the team worked to reinforce their positions, Georgiy and Jennifer moved to a more secure area of the headquarters. Jennifer could see the strain on Georgiy's face and knew they needed to stay strong for each other and their team.

Suddenly, an explosion rocked the building, and the lights flickered. Alarms blared, signaling another breach. The rival faction had resumed their attack, and this time they were more determined than ever.

"We need to get to the mainframe and protect the anomaly," Jennifer said urgently. "Stay close to me, Georgiy."

They moved quickly through the corridors, encountering pockets of resistance. The rival operatives were relentless, their attacks growing more desperate and intense. The sounds of battle echoed around them, but Georgiy and Jennifer pressed on, their resolve unshaken.

As they approached the mainframe room, they saw a group of operatives attempting to breach the security door.Jennifer raised her weapon, ready to defend their position.

"Cover me!" she shouted to Georgiy.

Georgiy aimed his weapon and fired at the operatives, forcing them to take cover. Jennifer moved swiftly, her movements precise and controlled. She fired at the intruders, taking down several and pushing the rest back.

"Keep going!" Jennifer urged. "We're almost there!"

They reached the mainframe room just as the security door began to buckle under the pressure. Dr. Li was already inside, coordinating the defense and ensuring that the anomaly remained stable.

"We need to hold this position!" Dr. Li shouted. "They can't get through here!"

Jennifer and Georgiy joined the defense, their determination unwavering. The rival operatives launched a relentless assault, but the IISF team fought back with everything they had.

In another part of the facility, Dr. Fernandez and Dr. Moreno were working to maintain the stability of the anomaly. The console in front of them beeped with warnings as the rift fluctuated under the stress of the ongoing battle.

"Adjust the phase alignment!" Dr. Fernandez shouted over the alarms.

Dr. Moreno's hands flew over the controls. "I'm on it! We need to stabilize the energy levels or the whole thing could collapse!"

The ground shook with the force of nearby explosions. Dr. Fernandez glanced at the monitor, his face set with grim determination. "We can't let them take Georgiy. We have to hold it together."

Back at the mainframe room, the battle intensified. The rival faction was making a final push to breach the defenses. Jennifer and Georgiy fought side by side, their actions coordinated and effective.

Suddenly, a burst of gunfire forced them to take cover behind a console. Georgiy looked at Jennifer, his face etched with concern. "We can't hold them off much longer."

Jennifer's eyes were filled with determination. "We have to. For the team, for the future. We can't let them win."

As the operatives pressed their attack, Jennifer saw an opportunity. She turned to Georgiy, her voice urgent."I'm going to create a distraction. When I do, you need to get to the anomaly and help Dr. Fernandez and Dr. Moreno stabilize it."

Georgiy's eyes widened. "Jennifer, that's too dangerous!"

Jennifer squeezed his hand, her gaze unwavering. "Trust me. We have to protect the anomaly at all costs.Go!"

Before Georgiy could protest, Jennifer moved out from behind the console, drawing the operatives' fire. She darted between cover points, her movements quick and agile. The distraction worked, and the operatives' focus shifted to her.

Taking advantage of the distraction, Georgiy made his way to the anomaly room, his heart pounding. He reached the room just as Dr. Fernandez and Dr. Moreno were making final adjustments to stabilize the rift.

"We need to lock down the energy levels now!" Dr. Fernandez shouted.

Georgiy joined them, his hands moving over the controls. "Let's do this."

The ground shook again, and the lights flickered as the rift began to stabilize. The console beeped with warnings, but the team pressed on, their determination unshaken.

In the mainframe room, Jennifer continued to hold off the operatives, her actions buying the team precious time. She moved with precision, her weapon discharging bursts of energy that forced the intruders back.

But the rival faction was relentless, and Jennifer knew she couldn't hold them off forever. Just as the security door began to buckle under the pressure, reinforcements arrived. Dr. Li had coordinated a counterattack, and the additional security personnel pushed the operatives back, securing the area.

Jennifer collapsed against a wall, her breathing heavy but her spirit unbroken. She knew they had won a crucial victory, but the cost had been high.

Back in the anomaly room, the rift finally stabilized, the warnings on the console fading. Dr. Fernandez let out a sigh of relief. "We did it. The anomaly is stable."

Georgiy nodded, feeling a wave of exhaustion wash over him. "Thank you, both of you. We couldn't have done this without you."

Dr. Moreno smiled, her face lined with relief. "It was a team effort. We all made sacrifices today."

As they regrouped, the sounds of battle outside began to fade. The IISF team had repelled the rival faction, but the cost had been significant. Several team members were injured, and the headquarters had suffered damage.

Georgiy and Jennifer found each other in the aftermath, their bodies weary but their spirits unbroken. They had faced the threat head-on and emerged stronger for it.

"We did it," Georgiy said, his voice filled with relief.

Jennifer nodded, her eyes reflecting the same sentiment. "Together. Always."

Their embrace was a moment of solace amidst the chaos, a reminder of the strength they drew from each other and their shared commitment to their mission.

Chapter 32

The battle was over, but the sense of urgency and tension lingered in the air. The IISF headquarters bore the scars of the conflict: shattered glass, scorched walls, and debris littering the hallways. Security personnel moved through the facility, ensuring that all threats had been neutralized and attending to the wounded.

Georgiy and Jennifer walked through the aftermath, their hearts heavy with the toll the battle had taken. They stopped in the command center, where Dr. Li was coordinating the cleanup and recovery efforts.

"How are we looking?" Georgiy asked, his voice weary.

Dr. Li glanced up from the console, his expression grave. "We've sustained significant damage, but we're holding together. Several team members are injured, and we've lost some critical equipment. But the anomaly is stable, and we've repelled the attack."

Jennifer placed a reassuring hand on Georgiy's shoulder. "We'll rebuild, Georgiy. We've faced challenges before, and we've come out stronger."

Georgiy nodded, drawing strength from her words. "What about the rival faction? Do we know more about their motivations?"

Dr. Li sighed, rubbing his temples. "We've been analyzing the data we captured during the attack. It's clear that the faction within the IISF has deep political motivations. They see our research and the advancements we're making as a threat to their own power and influence. Their goal was to undermine our efforts and seize control of our work."

Dr. Patel joined them, holding a stack of documents and a data pad. "We've found encrypted messages and hidden documents that reveal a complex web of power struggles within the IISF. There are high-ranking officials who have been secretly supporting the rival faction, providing them with resources and intelligence."

Georgiy felt a wave of anger and frustration. "All this time, they've been working against us from within. We need to root out these traitors and ensure that our work continues without interference."

Jennifer nodded in agreement. "We'll need to conduct a thorough investigation and strengthen our security measures. We can't afford to let this happen again."

As the team worked to uncover more information about the rival faction, Georgiy and Jennifer found a moment of quiet in the rooftop garden. The stars above them shone brightly, a reminder of the vastness of the universe and the importance of their work.

"Jennifer," Georgiy began, taking her hand in his, "this has been the most challenging time of my life, but it's also been the most rewarding. I've found a purpose here, and I've found you. I want to face whatever comes next together."

Jennifer's eyes softened, and she smiled. "I feel the same way, Georgiy. We've been through so much, and I can't imagine facing the future without you by my side. Whatever challenges come our way, we'll face them together."

Their kiss was a promise, a vow to support each other through the trials and triumphs that lay ahead.

Back in the command center, the team continued to piece together the rival faction's plans. Dr. Li, Dr. Patel, Dr. Fernandez, and Dr. Moreno worked tirelessly, analyzing data and coordinating the recovery efforts.

"We've identified several key figures within the IISF who have been supporting the rival faction," Dr. Patel said, pointing to a list of names on the data pad. "These individuals have been using their positions to gather intelligence and provide resources to the faction."

Dr. Li nodded, his expression resolute. "We need to confront these traitors and ensure that they can't undermine our work any further. We'll need to bring this information to the highest levels of the IISF and push for a thorough investigation."

Georgiy and Jennifer joined the discussion, their resolve strengthened by their shared commitment to their mission and each other.

"We'll need to be cautious," Georgiy said. "These individuals are well-placed and have significant influence. But we can't let them derail our efforts. Our work is too important."

Jennifer added, "We'll also need to rebuild and strengthen our defenses. The rival faction won't give up easily, and we need to be prepared for any future attacks."

As the team planned their next steps, the sense of unity and determination was palpable. They had faced a formidable enemy and emerged victorious, but the challenges ahead would require all their strength and resilience.

That evening, Georgiy and Jennifer sat together, reflecting on the day's events and the path ahead. The bond between them had grown stronger through the trials they had faced, and they drew comfort from each other's presence.

"Georgiy," Jennifer said softly, "we've come so far, and we've achieved so much. But there's still so much more to do. I believe in us and in our mission. We'll continue to push the boundaries of science and make a difference in this world."

Georgiy smiled, his heart filled with love and determination. "I believe in us too, Jennifer. Together, we can face any challenge and create a brighter future."

As they held each other under the starlit sky, they knew that their journey was far from over. The road ahead would be filled with obstacles, but they were ready to face them together, united by their love and their shared vision for the future.

Chapter 33

T he days following the battle were filled with both rebuilding and reflection. The IISF headquarters buzzed with activity as the team worked tirelessly to repair the damage and strengthen their defenses. The sense of urgency was tempered by a renewed sense of purpose and unity.

Georgiy and Jennifer spent their days overseeing the reconstruction efforts and their evenings planning for the future. The bond between them had grown stronger through the trials they had faced, and they drew strength from each other's presence.

In the main conference room, the core team gathered to discuss their progress and plan their next steps. Dr. Li stood at the head of the table, his expression determined.

"We've made significant progress in securing the facility and repairing the damage," he began. "But we need to ensure that we're prepared for any future threats. Strengthening our defenses and improving our security protocols is our top priority."

Dr. Patel nodded in agreement. "We also need to continue our investigation into the rival faction. Identifying and removing any remaining threats within the IISF is crucial."

Dr. Fernandez and Dr. Moreno provided updates on their work to stabilize the anomaly and protect their research. "The anomaly is stable, and we've implemented additional safeguards to prevent any further disruptions," Dr. Fernandez reported. "Our focus now is on advancing our research and exploring new possibilities."

Georgiy listened intently, feeling a renewed sense of hope. "Our work is more important than ever. We've shown that we can overcome challenges and continue pushing the boundaries of science. Let's use this as an opportunity to strengthen our team and our mission."

Jennifer smiled at him, her eyes filled with pride. "Together, we can achieve anything. Let's keep moving forward and building a brighter future."

As the weeks passed, the IISF team worked diligently to rebuild and improve their facility. Security measures were enhanced, new protocols were implemented, and the team grew closer and more united than ever.

Georgiy and Jennifer found moments of quiet amidst the hustle and bustle, their relationship deepening with each passing day. They would often retreat to the rooftop garden in the evenings, finding solace in each other's company and the beauty of the night sky.

One evening, as they sat together under the stars, Jennifer turned to Georgiy, her expression serious but filled with warmth. "Georgiy, we've been through so much together, and I can't imagine facing the future without you. I want us to continue this journey together, no matter what challenges come our way."

Georgiy took her hand in his, his heart swelling with love. "Jennifer, I feel the same way. You've become an integral part of my life, and I want to face whatever comes together. Our work, our mission, and our love give me hope for the future."

Their kiss was a promise, a vow to support each other through the trials and triumphs that lay ahead. As they held each other under the starlit sky, they knew that their journey was far from over, but they were ready to face it together.

In the weeks that followed, the IISF team made significant strides in their research and exploration. The advancements they achieved were groundbreaking, pushing the boundaries of science and opening up new possibilities for the future.

Georgiy and Jennifer worked closely with the team, their leadership and dedication inspiring everyone around them. The sense of unity and purpose that had grown from their shared experiences was palpable, and the team's determination to succeed was stronger than ever.

One afternoon, as Georgiy and Jennifer reviewed the latest data from their experiments, Dr. Li entered the room with a look of excitement. "We've made a major breakthrough," he announced. "Our latest tests have shown that we can stabilize the anomaly even further and potentially extend the time frame of Georgiy's stay."

Georgiy's eyes widened with surprise and hope. "That's incredible news. How soon can we implement these changes?"

Dr. Li smiled. "We're working on it now. With your help, we can begin the next phase of our research and continue making strides in our work."

Jennifer squeezed Georgiy's hand, her eyes shining with excitement. "This is just the beginning, Georgiy. We have so much more to achieve."

As the team gathered to celebrate their progress and plan their next steps, the sense of optimism and determination was undeniable. They had faced formidable challenges and emerged stronger for it, and their commitment to their mission and each other had never been stronger.

That evening, Georgiy and Jennifer stood on the rooftop garden, looking out over the city. The stars above them were a reminder of the endless possibilities that lay ahead.

"Jennifer," Georgiy said softly, "we've come so far, and we have so much more to do. I'm excited about the future and what we can achieve together."

Jennifer smiled, her eyes filled with love and determination. "Me too, Georgiy. We'll face whatever comes our way and continue to push the boundaries of science and exploration. Together, we can achieve anything."

As they held each other under the starlit sky, they knew that their journey was just beginning. The challenges they had faced had only strengthened their resolve and deepened their bond. Together, they were ready to build a brighter future, filled with endless possibilities and unwavering hope.

Chapter 34

Georgiy woke up early, feeling a sense of anticipation. The previous night had been filled with dreams of the future, dreams where he and Jennifer continued their groundbreaking work without the looming threat of the rival faction. He dressed quickly and headed to the main conference room, where the core team was already gathering.

Dr. Li greeted him with a nod. "Good morning, Georgiy. We have some important updates. Please take a seat."

Georgiy joined Jennifer and the others at the table. The room was filled with an air of urgency as Dr. Li began the briefing.

"We've been analyzing the data and documents we recovered during the recent confrontation," Dr. Li said, his tone serious. "What we've found is both troubling and revealing."

Dr. Patel projected a series of documents and encrypted messages onto the screen. "These files contain detailed plans and communications from the rival faction. They reveal a coordinated effort to undermine our work and take control of the IISF."

Georgiy leaned forward, studying the documents. The messages were filled with technical jargon and strategic plans, outlining various methods to sabotage the IISF's efforts. His eyes scanned the text, trying to absorb as much information as possible.

"Who is behind this?" Georgiy asked, his voice tense.

Dr. Moreno pointed to a name that appeared frequently in the communications. "It appears that a high-ranking official within the IISF, Director Ivanov, has been secretly orchestrating the attacks. He's been using his position to gather intelligence and provide resources to the rival faction."

Jennifer's eyes widened in shock. "Ivanov? He's always been a staunch supporter of our work. This betrayal runs deep."

Dr. Fernandez nodded. "He's been playing both sides, supporting our efforts publicly while secretly working against us. His goal is to seize control of our research and use it for his own gain."

Georgiy felt a surge of anger. "We need to confront Ivanov and expose his actions. This cannot continue."

Dr. Li agreed. "We'll need to proceed carefully. Ivanov has significant influence and resources. We need to gather more evidence and plan our next steps strategically."

The team spent the next several hours poring over the documents and decrypting messages. The extent of Ivanov's betrayal became increasingly clear, and the team's resolve to stop him grew stronger.

As they worked, the room was filled with the hum of computers and the soft murmur of voices discussing their findings. Georgiy and Jennifer worked side by side, their determination mirrored in each other's eyes.

"Look at this," Jennifer said, pointing to a particularly damning piece of evidence. "Ivanov has been coordinating with external operatives. He's been funneling information and resources to them for months."

Georgiy nodded, his jaw clenched. "This explains how they've been able to stay one step ahead of us. Ivanov's been feeding them our plans and strategies."

Dr. Li approached, holding a stack of newly decrypted documents. "We need to compile all of this evidence and prepare a report for the IISF board. They need to see the full extent of Ivanov's betrayal."

The team worked late into the night, their focus unwavering. By the time they had finished, they had compiled a comprehensive report detailing Ivanov's actions and the threat posed by the rival faction.

As the day turned to night, Georgiy and Jennifer took a break, finding a moment of quiet in the rooftop garden. The stars above them provided a sense of calm amidst the turmoil.

"We'll get through this, Georgiy," Jennifer said, her voice filled with determination. "We've faced challenges before, and we'll overcome this one too."

Georgiy nodded, taking her hand in his. "Together, we can face anything. We'll expose Ivanov and ensure that our work continues without interference."

Their resolve strengthened by each other's presence, they returned to the task at hand, ready to face whatever came next.

Chapter 35

The following morning, the core team reconvened to discuss their findings and plan their next steps. The conference room was filled with tension as they reviewed the evidence against Ivanov.

Dr. Li began the meeting with a sense of urgency. "We've uncovered significant evidence of Ivanov's betrayal, but there's more to this than we initially thought," he said. "It's likely that he has allies within our ranks, feeding him information and undermining our efforts."

Jennifer nodded, her expression grim. "We need to identify and neutralize any moles within the IISF. If we don't, our work and our safety will continue to be at risk."

Dr. Fernandez suggested a covert investigation. "We should start by monitoring communications and observing any suspicious behavior. We need to be discreet and methodical in our approach."

The team agreed, and they set up a covert operation to identify the mole. Surveillance equipment was installed, and trusted members of the team were assigned to monitor communications and report any unusual activity.

As the days passed, tension within the IISF grew. The sense of mistrust was palpable, and everyone was on high alert. Georgiy and Jennifer worked closely with Dr. Li and the others, reviewing the surveillance footage and analyzing the data.

One evening, as Georgiy was reviewing a series of encrypted messages, he noticed a pattern. The messages were coming from someone within the research division, someone with access to sensitive information.

"Jennifer, take a look at this," he said, calling her over. "These messages are being sent from within our own team."

Jennifer's eyes narrowed as she studied the data. "We need to confront this person and find out what they know. But we have to be careful. If they realize we're onto them, they might try to destroy evidence or escape."

The team devised a plan to confront the suspected mole without alerting them. Dr. Li coordinated with security to ensure that the person would be apprehended quickly and discreetly.

The following day, they put their plan into action. Georgiy and Jennifer, along with Dr. Li and the security team, approached the suspected mole in the research lab. The tension in the room was thick as they made their move.

"Dr. Martin," Dr. Li began, his voice steady, "we need to speak with you."

Dr. Martin looked up from his work, a flicker of panic in his eyes. "What is this about?"

Jennifer stepped forward, her expression firm. "We've discovered evidence that you've been communicating with Ivanov and the rival faction. We need to know the extent of your involvement."

Dr. Martin's face went pale, and he glanced around the room as if looking for an escape. The security team moved in, ensuring that he couldn't flee.

"It's over, Martin," Georgiy said quietly. "Tell us everything."

Dr. Martin sighed, his shoulders slumping in defeat. "I never wanted to hurt anyone. Ivanov promised me power and influence. He said we could achieve more if we took control of the IISF. I was a fool to believe him."

The team listened as Dr. Martin detailed his involvement and the information he had passed to Ivanov. The betrayal cut deep, but the team was determined to move forward and ensure that their work remained secure.

As they gathered more information from Dr. Martin, they realized the extent of the rival faction's infiltration. Ivanov's network was more extensive than they had anticipated, and several other members of the IISF were implicated in the conspiracy.

Dr. Li addressed the team, his voice filled with resolve. "We need to act quickly and decisively. We'll gather all the evidence we can and present it to the IISF board. Ivanov and his allies must be held accountable."

Georgiy and Jennifer exchanged a determined look. "We'll be ready," Jennifer said. "We must protect our work and our future."

As the team continued their covert investigation, they worked tirelessly to uncover the full extent of Ivanov's network. The sense of unity and determination was stronger than ever, and they knew that they were fighting for the future of their research and their mission.

The days that followed were filled with tension and anticipation. The team gathered evidence, monitored communications, and prepared for the confrontation with Ivanov and his allies. The sense of mistrust within the IISF began to dissipate as the team's efforts brought them closer together.

One evening, as Georgiy and Jennifer reviewed the latest findings, they found a moment of quiet in the rooftop garden. The stars above them provided a sense of calm amidst the turmoil.

"Jennifer," Georgiy said softly, taking her hand in his, "we've come so far, and we've faced so many challenges. But I believe in us and in our mission. We'll get through this together."

Jennifer smiled, her eyes filled with determination. "I believe in us too, Georgiy. Together, we can face anything."

Their kiss was a promise, a vow to support each other through the trials and triumphs that lay ahead. As they held each other under the starlit sky, they knew that their journey was far from over, but they were ready to face it together.

Chapter 36

With Dr. Martin's confession, the team had the evidence they needed to confront Ivanov. Dr. Li coordinated with the highest levels of the IISF, ensuring they had the support needed to take down the traitor.

The following day, the team gathered in the command center to finalize their plan. The room was filled with a mix of anticipation and determination.

Dr. Li stood at the head of the table, his expression resolute. "We have everything we need to expose Ivanov and his allies. Our priority is to apprehend them quickly and prevent any further damage to our work."

Jennifer nodded. "Security is in place, and we have backup from the highest levels of the IISF. We need to act swiftly and decisively."

Dr. Fernandez added, "We've also secured the critical areas of our research. No matter what happens, the anomaly and our data will be protected."

Georgiy felt a surge of determination. "Let's do this."

The team moved with precision, each member knowing their role in the operation. Security forces were placed on high alert, and the team prepared for the confrontation. Georgiy and Jennifer stood together, ready to face whatever came next.

As they approached Ivanov's office, the tension was palpable. Dr. Li led the way, flanked by security personnel. They burst into the office, catching Ivanov by surprise.

"Ivanov, it's over," Dr. Li said firmly. "We have evidence of your betrayal. You're under arrest."

Ivanov's face twisted with anger and desperation. "You have no idea what you're doing! I was trying to save the IISF, to bring it to its true potential!"

Georgiy stepped forward, his voice calm but resolute. "Your actions have endangered us all. You betrayed our trust and our mission."

Ivanov's eyes flickered with fury as he reached for a hidden weapon. The security team reacted quickly, subduing him and ensuring he couldn't cause any further harm.

As they secured Ivanov and began searching his office, they uncovered critical information about the rival faction's next move. Plans for another attack were detailed in encrypted files, revealing the extent of their determination to take control of the IISF.

Dr. Li turned to the team, his expression serious. "We need to prepare for this next attack. They won't stop until they've achieved their goals. But now, we have the upper hand. We know their plans, and we can use this to our advantage."

Georgiy and Jennifer exchanged a determined look. "We'll be ready," Jennifer said. "Let's make sure they can't threaten our work again."

The team worked tirelessly, decrypting the files and analyzing the rival faction's plans. They coordinated with security forces, ensuring every possible angle was covered.

In the following days, the IISF headquarters buzzed with activity. Georgiy and Jennifer oversaw the preparations, ensuring that their research remained protected and that the team was ready for whatever came next.

One evening, as they reviewed the latest security protocols, Jennifer looked at Georgiy, her expression thoughtful. "We've come a long way, Georgiy. There's still so much to do, but I'm confident we can handle whatever comes our way."

Georgiy smiled, feeling a deep sense of connection with her. "I'm confident too. We're stronger together, and we'll keep pushing forward."

As they worked late into the night, the sense of unity and determination among the team grew stronger. They knew the challenges ahead would be formidable, but they were ready to face them together.

Chapter 37

The information extracted from Ivanov's files painted a grim picture of the rival faction's ambitions. They were planning a large-scale attack on the IISF headquarters, intending to seize control of the research and the temporal anomaly. The team knew they had to act swiftly and strategically to protect their work and ensure the safety of everyone involved.

The core team gathered in the command center to devise a plan. The room was filled with maps, data projections, and a palpable sense of urgency.

Dr. Li began the briefing, his voice steady but intense. "Based on the decrypted files, the rival faction is planning their attack within the next 48 hours. Their goal is to take control of our facility and capture key personnel, including Dr. Garbuz."

Jennifer nodded, her expression resolute. "We need to fortify our defenses and ensure that all critical areas are protected. This includes the mainframe, the anomaly lab, and our research archives."

Dr. Fernandez added, "We should also establish multiple fallback positions throughout the facility. If they manage to breach our defenses, we need to be able to regroup and continue the fight."

Georgiy spoke up, his voice filled with determination. "What can I do to help?"

Dr. Li looked at him with respect. "Your knowledge of the anomaly and the research is invaluable. We need you to work with Dr. Fernandez and Dr. Moreno to ensure the anomaly remains stable and protected."

Jennifer squeezed Georgiy's hand. "We also need to make sure you're safe. Your safety is crucial to our mission."

The team spent the next several hours fortifying their positions and coordinating their defense strategy. Security personnel were deployed throughout the facility, surveillance systems were enhanced, and emergency protocols were reviewed and updated.

As the sun set, the team gathered for a final briefing. Dr. Li outlined the plan, his voice firm and confident. "Our primary objective is to protect the anomaly and our research. We'll be monitoring all entry points and have teams ready to respond to any breach. Stay alert, stay focused, and we'll get through this."

Georgiy and Jennifer took a moment to themselves before the expected confrontation. They stood on the rooftop garden, the stars above them providing a moment of peace before the storm.

"Georgiy," Jennifer began, her voice soft but filled with resolve, "we've faced so much together, and I know we can handle this too. Just remember, we're not alone. We have a strong team, and we're all in this together."

Georgiy nodded, his heart swelling with affection and determination. "I know, Jennifer. And no matter what happens, we'll face it head-on. Our work is too important to let anything stop us."

Their embrace was a silent vow, a promise to support each other through the trials ahead. As they held each other under the starlit sky, they knew that their journey was far from over, but they were ready to face it together.

The following day was filled with a tense calm as the team awaited the inevitable attack. Security personnel patrolled the halls, and surveillance monitors displayed live feeds from every corner of the facility.

In the anomaly lab, Georgiy worked closely with Dr. Fernandez and Dr. Moreno to ensure the stability of the temporal anomaly. The humming of machines and the soft beeping of monitors filled the room as they double-checked every system.

"We've reinforced the containment field and added additional layers of security," Dr. Fernandez explained. "If they try to tamper with the anomaly, they'll have a hard time getting through."

Dr. Moreno nodded in agreement. "We've also set up a remote monitoring system. If we need to evacuate, we can still keep an eye on the anomaly and manage its stability from a secure location."

Georgiy felt a sense of relief knowing that the anomaly was well-protected. "Thank you both. This gives me confidence that we can keep our work safe."

Meanwhile, Jennifer coordinated with the security teams, ensuring that all personnel were briefed and ready. She moved through the facility with calm authority, her presence reassuring to everyone around her.

As the hours passed, the tension grew thicker. The team was ready, but the uncertainty of when the attack would come weighed heavily on their minds.

In the command center, Dr. Li monitored the surveillance feeds, his eyes scanning for any sign of the rival faction. "Stay sharp, everyone," he said over the comms. "We need to be ready to respond at a moment's notice."

The anticipation was almost unbearable, but the team remained focused and determined. They had prepared as best they could, and now they were ready to defend their work and their future.

Chapter 38

The facility was eerily quiet, the calm before the storm. The team was stationed at their posts, their senses heightened as they awaited the impending attack. Georgiy stood in the anomaly lab with Dr. Fernandez and Dr. Moreno, their eyes glued to the monitors.

In the command center, Dr. Li and Jennifer coordinated the defense. Surveillance feeds displayed every corner of the facility, the screens flickering with activity.

Suddenly, an alarm blared, shattering the silence. The surveillance monitors lit up with movement as figures appeared at the perimeter.

"They're here," Dr. Li announced over the comms. "Everyone, to your positions."

The rival faction moved with military precision, breaching the outer defenses with alarming speed. Security personnel engaged them immediately, the sounds of gunfire and explosions echoing through the facility.

"Sector 4 breach!" a security officer shouted. "We need reinforcements!"

Jennifer responded quickly, her voice steady and commanding. "Reinforcements are on their way. Hold the line!"

Georgiy, watching the chaos unfold on the monitors, felt a surge of determination. "We need to make sure the anomaly stays stable," he said to Dr. Fernandez and Dr. Moreno.

They nodded, their faces set with resolve. "We're ready," Dr. Fernandez replied, his hands flying over the controls to adjust the containment field.

In the corridors, the battle raged on. Security personnel and rival operatives clashed, the air thick with smoke and the acrid smell of burning circuitry. The rival faction was relentless, their attacks coordinated and fierce.

Jennifer moved through the facility, directing teams and ensuring that critical areas were defended. She fired at approaching operatives, her movements swift and precise.

"Georgiy, how's the anomaly holding?" she called over the comms.

"We're stable for now," Georgiy replied, his voice tense. "But we need to keep a close watch. Any disruption could be catastrophic."

As the battle intensified, the rival faction made a push towards the mainframe. Dr. Li and his team were prepared, fortified behind barricades and ready to defend their position.

"They're trying to access the mainframe!" Dr. Li shouted. "We need to hold them off!"

The security team responded with a barrage of gunfire, forcing the operatives to take cover. The rival faction was relentless, but the IISF team's determination was stronger.

In the anomaly lab, Georgiy and his team worked tirelessly to maintain stability. The console beeped with warnings as the energy levels fluctuated.

"Adjust the phase alignment," Dr. Moreno instructed, her voice calm but urgent. "We need to compensate for the disruptions."

Georgiy's hands moved swiftly over the controls. "We can't let them get to the anomaly. We need to keep it stable."

Meanwhile, Jennifer led a team to reinforce the defenses at the mainframe. The rival operatives were gaining ground, their attacks growing more desperate.

"We need to push them back!" Jennifer shouted. "Don't let them breach the mainframe!"

The security personnel fought with fierce resolve, their determination unwavering. Jennifer fired at the operatives, hitting one and forcing the others to retreat.

"We're holding, but we need more support!" a security officer called out.

Jennifer coordinated with the command center, directing additional forces to their position. The rival faction was relentless, but the IISF team's unity and determination proved to be their greatest strength.

In the anomaly lab, the situation grew more tense. The energy levels were spiking, and the containment field was straining under the pressure.

"We're reaching critical levels," Dr. Fernandez warned. "We need to stabilize the field now!"

Georgiy nodded, his face set with determination. "We can do this. Adjust the energy flow and reinforce the field."

As they worked, the ground shook with the force of nearby explosions. The rival faction was throwing everything they had at the facility, but the IISF team held their ground.

"Jennifer, we need to stabilize the anomaly now," Georgiy called over the comms. "We're running out of time."

"We're on it," Jennifer replied. "Stay focused and keep it together."

The battle reached its peak as the rival faction launched a final, desperate assault. The air was filled with the sounds of gunfire and explosions, the facility shaking with the intensity of the conflict.

In the command center, Dr. Li coordinated the defense, his voice calm but commanding. "Sector 5, hold your position. Mainframe team, prepare for a counterattack."

The security personnel responded with precision, their movements coordinated and efficient. They held the line, pushing back the intruders with a combination of strategy and sheer determination.

In the anomaly lab, Georgiy and his team made the final adjustments to stabilize the rift. The energy levels spiked, and the ground shook violently.

"Hold on!" Dr. Fernandez shouted. "We're almost there!"

Georgiy focused on the controls, his hands moving swiftly. The console beeped with warnings, but he remained calm and determined.

With a final adjustment, the energy levels began to stabilize, and the rift closed. The humming of the machines faded, and the lab fell silent.

"We did it," Georgiy said, letting out a sigh of relief. "The anomaly is stable."

Dr. Moreno smiled, her face lined with exhaustion but filled with relief. "Great work, everyone. We held it together."

Back in the mainframe, Jennifer and her team pushed the rival operatives back, securing their position. The rival faction's attacks grew more desperate, but the IISF team's unity and determination proved to be their greatest strength.

"We've got them on the run!" Jennifer shouted. "Keep pushing!"

The security personnel pressed forward, driving the operatives back and securing the facility. The sounds of battle gradually faded, replaced by the hum of the facility's systems coming back online.

In the command center, Dr. Li monitored the situation, his face filled with a sense of accomplishment. "We did it. The facility is secure."

As the dust settled, the IISF team regrouped, their bodies weary but their spirits unbroken. They had faced the threat head-on and emerged victorious.

Georgiy and Jennifer found each other amidst the aftermath, their faces reflecting the same sense of relief and determination.

"We did it," Georgiy said, his voice filled with emotion.

Jennifer nodded, her eyes shining with pride. "We did. And we'll keep pushing forward, no matter what."

Their embrace was a moment of solace amidst the chaos, a reminder of the strength they drew from each other and their shared commitment to their mission.

Chapter 39

The battle was over, and the air in the IISF headquarters was filled with a mixture of relief and triumph. The team had fought valiantly to protect their research and their future, and their hard work had paid off. As the dust settled, the members of the IISF gathered in the central atrium to celebrate their victory.

Banners and decorations adorned the space, and a sense of camaraderie and accomplishment filled the room. Georgiy and Jennifer stood together, surrounded by their colleagues, each of them reflecting on the journey that had brought them to this moment.

Dr. Li raised a glass, his voice carrying through the atrium. "To our victory and to everyone who made it possible. We have faced incredible challenges, and we have overcome them together. Let us honor those who sacrificed so much for our cause and look forward to the bright future we are building."

The team raised their glasses in a toast, the clinking of crystal echoing through the atrium. Georgiy looked around at the faces of his friends and colleagues, feeling a deep sense of pride and gratitude. The journey had been long and arduous, but they had achieved something remarkable.

Dr. Fernandez approached Georgiy and Jennifer, a smile on his face. "We did it, Georgiy. We protected our work and our future. This is a moment to celebrate."

Jennifer nodded, her eyes shining with pride. "We couldn't have done it without each other. This team, this family, has accomplished something incredible."

As the celebration continued, Georgiy found himself reflecting on the sacrifices that had been made along the way. He thought of the friends and colleagues who had given everything for their mission, and he felt a pang of sorrow amidst the joy of their victory.

Dr. Moreno joined them, her expression thoughtful. "We've come so far, and we've achieved so much. But we must also remember those who aren't with us today. Their contributions and sacrifices have paved the way for our success."

Georgiy nodded, feeling the weight of her words. "We owe it to them to continue our work and to honor their legacy. This is only the beginning."

The team spent the evening sharing stories and memories, reflecting on the challenges they had faced and the triumphs they had achieved. The atmosphere was filled with laughter and camaraderie, a testament to the strong bonds that had been forged through their shared journey.

As the celebration began to wind down, Georgiy and Jennifer found a quiet moment together. They stood on the balcony overlooking the atrium, the stars twinkling above them.

"This has been an incredible journey, Jennifer," Georgiy said softly. "I'm so grateful to have been a part of it, and to have shared it with you."

Jennifer smiled, her eyes filled with warmth. "It's been an honor, Georgiy. We've faced so much together, and we've come out stronger for it. I wouldn't trade this experience for anything."

Their conversation was interrupted by Dr. Li, who approached with a serious expression. "Georgiy, Jennifer, there's something we need to discuss. It's important."

They followed Dr. Li to the command center, where the rest of the core team was already gathered. The atmosphere had shifted from celebration to concern, and Georgiy felt a knot of tension in his stomach.

Dr. Li began, his voice somber. "We've discovered something about the temporal anomaly. It appears that Georgiy's time travel is coming to an end. The anomaly is stabilizing, and it will soon transport him back to the past."

The room fell silent as the weight of Dr. Li's words sank in. Georgiy felt a sense of shock and disbelief. He had known that his time in the future was temporary, but the reality of his impending departure hit him hard.

Jennifer's face paled, her eyes wide with shock. "How long do we have?"

Dr. Li looked at the data on the screen. "A few days at most. We need to prepare for Georgiy's return to the past."

The revelation cast a shadow over the celebration, and the team was left to grapple with the implications of Georgiy's impending departure. The victory they had achieved felt bittersweet, and the future suddenly seemed uncertain.

As Georgiy and Jennifer stood together, their hands clasped tightly, they knew that the days ahead would be filled with difficult decisions and emotional farewells. The journey was far from over, and they would face it together, come what may.

Chapter 40

The days following the celebration were filled with an uneasy tension. The revelation of Georgiy's impending departure loomed over the IISF like a dark cloud. The team tried to carry on with their work, but the knowledge that their friend and colleague would soon be leaving weighed heavily on their hearts.

Georgiy and Jennifer found it difficult to focus, their minds constantly drifting back to the harsh reality they were facing. They spent more time together, finding solace in each other's presence, but the strain on their relationship was becoming evident.

One afternoon, as they were working in the lab, Georgiy noticed Jennifer's distracted expression. He put down his work and approached her, his concern evident.

"Jennifer, are you okay?" he asked gently.

Jennifer looked up, her eyes filled with a mix of sadness and frustration. "I'm trying to be, Georgiy, but it's hard. Knowing that you'll be leaving soon... it's tearing me apart."

Georgiy took her hand in his, feeling the same pain. "I know, Jennifer. It's hard for me too. But we have to make the most of the time we have left."

She pulled her hand away, her voice rising with emotion. "How am I supposed to do that? Every moment we spend together just reminds me that it's all going to end. How can I be okay with that?"

Georgiy felt a pang of guilt and helplessness. "I don't have any easy answers. All I know is that I don't want to spend these last days apart, pushing each other away because it hurts too much. We need to stay strong, for each other and for the team."

Jennifer's eyes filled with tears, and she turned away, her shoulders shaking with silent sobs. Georgiy moved closer, wrapping his arms around her and holding her tightly.

"I'm here, Jennifer," he whispered. "I'm here with you now."

The strain on their relationship continued to grow as the days passed. The team noticed the tension between Georgiy and Jennifer, but no one knew how to help. The impending separation cast a shadow over their work, and even the smallest tasks felt heavy with the weight of the unknown.

Dr. Li called a meeting to discuss their next steps. The core team gathered in the conference room, their faces etched with worry.

"We need to prepare for Georgiy's departure," Dr. Li began, his voice steady but tinged with sadness. "We have to ensure that his return to the past is as smooth as possible and that our research remains secure."

Dr. Fernandez nodded. "We should document everything we've done, so Georgiy can take that knowledge back with him. It will help him continue his work in the past."

Dr. Moreno added, "We also need to consider the emotional impact this will have on the team. We've all grown close to Georgiy, and his departure will be difficult for everyone."

Jennifer sat quietly, her mind racing with thoughts of the future. She felt torn between her duty to the team and her personal pain. She wanted to be strong, but the prospect of losing Georgiy was overwhelming.

After the meeting, Georgiy and Jennifer walked together to the rooftop garden, their favorite place to find peace. The stars twinkled above them, a reminder of the vastness of the universe and the smallness of their time together.

"Jennifer," Georgiy began softly, "I know this is incredibly hard. But we have to find a way to get through this. We've faced so many challenges together, and we've always come out stronger."

Jennifer looked up at the stars, her eyes filled with unshed tears. "I don't know if I can do this, Georgiy. Every part of me wants to fight this, to find a way to keep you here."

Georgiy gently turned her to face him, his hands resting on her shoulders. "We have to accept what we can't change. But that doesn't mean we have to let it break us. We can still make these last days meaningful. We can still cherish our time together."

She nodded slowly, leaning into his embrace. "I'll try, Georgiy. I'll try to be strong."

They held each other in the quiet night, the weight of the impending separation pressing down on them. They knew the days ahead would be filled with pain and uncertainty, but they were determined to face it together, no matter how difficult it would be.

Chapter 41

The days that followed were fraught with tension and emotional turmoil. The team continued their work, but the impending separation cast a long shadow over everything they did. Georgiy and Jennifer, once inseparable, found themselves drifting apart, each grappling with their own fears and frustrations.

One morning, as they sat in the anomaly lab, Jennifer broke the silence that had settled between them. "Georgiy, I've been thinking... maybe it's better if we start to distance ourselves now. It might make it easier when the time comes."

Georgiy looked up, shock and hurt evident in his eyes. "Distance ourselves? Jennifer, I don't want to spend our remaining time apart. That will only make it harder."

Jennifer's face hardened, a defense mechanism against the pain she was feeling. "I'm just trying to find a way to cope, Georgiy. This isn't easy for me. Every moment with you is a reminder that I'm going to lose you."

Georgiy's voice softened, his heart aching at her words. "I know it's hard, Jennifer. But pushing each other away won't help. We need to face this together, not apart."

Jennifer turned away, tears streaming down her face. "I don't know how to do that, Georgiy. I don't know how to say goodbye."

The strain on their relationship became more apparent with each passing day. Their conversations grew shorter, filled with unspoken fears and unresolved tension. The team noticed the change, but respected their privacy, giving them space to navigate their emotions.

Dr. Li, sensing the growing distance between them, approached Georgiy in the lab one afternoon. "Georgiy, I've noticed that things have been difficult between you and Jennifer. It's understandable, given the circumstances. But you need to find a way to support each other through this."

Georgiy sighed, running a hand through his hair. "I know, Dr. Li. It's just... every time we talk about the future, it feels like we're tearing each other apart. I don't know how to fix it."

Dr. Li placed a reassuring hand on his shoulder. "You both care deeply for each other. That's clear to everyone. But sometimes, when we're faced with something as painful as this, we build walls to protect ourselves. Maybe you just need to find a way to break through those walls and be honest about your fears and hopes."

Georgiy nodded, appreciating Dr. Li's wisdom. "Thank you. I'll try to talk to her, really talk to her."

That evening, Georgiy found Jennifer in the rooftop garden, staring up at the stars. He approached her slowly, unsure of how to start the conversation.

"Jennifer," he began, his voice gentle, "we need to talk."

She turned to face him, her eyes weary but open. "I know, Georgiy. I've been avoiding it because it hurts too much. But you're right. We need to face this."

He took her hands in his, looking into her eyes. "I'm scared too, Jennifer. I'm scared of leaving you, of what will happen when I'm gone. But I don't want to waste our time together by pushing you away."

Jennifer's eyes filled with tears, but she didn't pull away. "I'm scared of losing you, Georgiy. Every part of me wants to find a way to keep you here, to fight the impossible. But I know that's not realistic."

Georgiy nodded, his own eyes misting. "We need to cherish the time we have left, even if it's hard. We've faced so much together, and we can face this too. I don't want our last days to be filled with regret and distance."

She leaned into his embrace, finding comfort in his presence. "You're right. I don't want to look back and regret the way we handled this. Let's make the most of our time, no matter how painful it might be."

They stood together, holding each other tightly, finding strength in their shared resolve. The journey ahead was uncertain and filled with heartache, but they were determined to face it together, side by side.

Chapter 42

The realization that Georgiy's time in the future was limited spurred the team into action. Determined to find a solution, they threw themselves into their work, exploring every possible avenue to stabilize the temporal anomaly and keep Georgiy from being transported back to the past.

The anomaly lab became the center of their efforts. The room buzzed with activity as Georgiy, Jennifer, Dr. Fernandez, and Dr. Moreno worked around the clock, their focus unwavering despite the emotional weight they carried.

"We need to find a way to stabilize the temporal field," Dr. Fernandez said, his voice tense but determined. "If we can extend its stability, we might be able to prevent the time jump."

Georgiy nodded, reviewing the latest data on the anomaly. "We've seen fluctuations in the field when we adjust the energy flow. Maybe if we can find the right balance, we can keep it stable."

Jennifer studied the monitors, her mind racing with possibilities. "What about using the harmonic frequencies we discovered last month? They seemed to have a stabilizing effect on the anomaly."

Dr. Moreno considered this, her brow furrowed in thought. "It's worth a try. Let's run a simulation to see how the frequencies interact with the current state of the anomaly."

The team worked tirelessly, running simulations and making adjustments to the containment field. The lab was filled with the hum of machines and the soft beeping of monitors, a constant reminder of the stakes.

As the hours turned into days, the strain began to take its toll. Exhaustion was etched on everyone's faces, but they refused to give up. The possibility of keeping Georgiy in the future was a beacon of hope that kept them going.

One evening, as they reviewed the latest simulation results, Georgiy felt a pang of despair. The data showed some improvement, but it wasn't enough to guarantee stability.

"We're running out of time," he said, his voice filled with frustration. "If we don't find a solution soon, it will be too late."

Jennifer placed a reassuring hand on his shoulder. "We're doing everything we can, Georgiy. We just have to keep pushing forward. We can't give up."

Dr. Fernandez joined them, his expression grim but resolute. "We've made progress, but we need to think outside the box. What haven't we tried yet?"

Georgiy took a deep breath, trying to clear his mind. "There might be one more thing we can do. If we can create a secondary containment field, it might provide the extra stability we need."

Dr. Moreno's eyes lit up with realization. "That's risky, but it could work. We'd need to calibrate the field precisely to avoid interfering with the primary containment."

Jennifer nodded, a spark of hope in her eyes. "Let's do it. We don't have anything to lose."

The team set to work, creating the secondary containment field and carefully calibrating it to support the primary field. The atmosphere in the lab was tense, every movement and adjustment carrying the weight of their hopes and fears.

As they activated the secondary field, the monitors flickered with data, showing the interaction between the two fields. The initial results were promising, but they needed to see if the stability could be maintained.

"Keep an eye on the energy levels," Georgiy instructed, his eyes fixed on the screen. "We need to make sure there are no fluctuations."

Minutes passed like hours as they watched the data. The tension was almost unbearable, but the team remained focused, their determination unshaken.

Finally, the data stabilized, showing a significant improvement in the containment field's stability. The anomaly appeared to be holding steady, the harmonic frequencies and secondary field working in tandem.

"We did it," Dr. Fernandez said, a note of triumph in his voice. "The field is stable."

Georgiy felt a surge of relief, but he knew they weren't out of the woods yet. "This is a step in the right direction, but we need to monitor it closely. Any changes could disrupt the stability."

Jennifer smiled, her eyes shining with hope. "We've bought ourselves some time. Let's make the most of it."

Over the next few days, the team continued to monitor the anomaly, making adjustments as needed to maintain stability. The atmosphere in the lab was a mix of cautious optimism and lingering tension, everyone aware that the situation could change at any moment.

Georgiy and Jennifer found moments of quiet amidst the chaos, their bond growing stronger as they faced the challenges together. They knew the road ahead would be difficult, but they were determined to see it through.

One evening, as they reviewed the latest data, Jennifer turned to Georgiy, her expression thoughtful. "Georgiy, no matter what happens, I want you to know how much you mean to me. You've changed my life in ways I never thought possible."

Georgiy took her hand, his eyes filled with emotion. "And you've changed mine, Jennifer. Whatever the future holds, I'm grateful for every moment we've shared."

Their words were a promise to each other, a vow to face whatever came next with courage and hope. As they held each other in the quiet of the lab, they knew that their journey was far from over, but they were ready to face it together, side by side.

Chapter 43

The anomaly's stability fluctuated, and despite their best efforts, the team realized they could not stop the inevitable. Georgiy would have to return to his own time. The atmosphere in the IISF headquarters was somber as the team prepared for his departure.

In the central atrium, the team gathered to say their goodbyes. The room was filled with the quiet murmur of conversations and the soft sounds of people trying to hold back tears. Georgiy stood with Jennifer by his side, both of them trying to savor every last moment together.

Dr. Li stepped forward, his face a mix of sadness and pride. "Georgiy, your contributions to our work and our lives have been immeasurable. We will carry forward your vision and honor your legacy."

Georgiy nodded, his voice thick with emotion. "Thank you, Dr. Li. Working with all of you has been the greatest honor of my life. I have seen a future filled with hope and innovation, and I know you will make it a reality."

Dr. Fernandez and Dr. Moreno approached, their expressions reflecting the deep bond they had formed with Georgiy. "You've been an inspiration to us all," Dr. Fernandez said. "We will continue to build on the foundation you've helped create."

Dr. Moreno added, "Your passion and dedication have driven us to new heights. We will never forget what you've done for us."

Georgiy embraced them both, feeling the weight of their words. "I will carry these memories with me always. Thank you for everything."

As the team members took their turns saying goodbye, Jennifer stood silently by Georgiy's side, her hand tightly clasped in his. When the farewells were nearly complete, she led him to the rooftop garden, the place where they had shared so many moments of peace and reflection.

The stars twinkled above them, a silent witness to their parting. Jennifer turned to Georgiy, her eyes filled with tears. "I don't know how to say goodbye," she whispered. "Every part of me wants to hold on and never let go."

Georgiy gently wiped away her tears, his own eyes shimmering with unshed tears. "This isn't goodbye, Jennifer. Our time together has changed me in ways I can't even begin to describe. No matter where I am, a part of you will always be with me."

She nodded, trying to hold back the sobs that threatened to escape. "I'll never forget you, Georgiy. You've shown me what it means to truly believe in something, to fight for a better future. I promise to carry on your work and keep your legacy alive."

They held each other tightly, the pain of their impending separation almost unbearable. "Remember," Georgiy said softly, "no matter what happens, we've made a difference. And that's something no one can take away from us."

Jennifer nodded, her heart breaking but filled with resolve. "I love you, Georgiy."

"I love you too, Jennifer," he replied, his voice choked with emotion.

As they returned to the atrium, the team gathered around Georgiy one last time. Dr. Li handed him a small device containing all their research and findings. "Take this with you, Georgiy. It's a piece of our future. Use it to continue your work in the past."

Georgiy accepted the device, feeling the weight of its importance. "Thank you. I will use this to build the future we've dreamed of."

The moment had come. The anomaly's energy began to pulse, signaling that the time for Georgiy's departure was near. He stood in the center of the room, the energy swirling around him, as the team watched with heavy hearts.

Jennifer stepped forward, her voice steady but filled with sorrow. "Goodbye, Georgiy. We'll carry your legacy forward."

Georgiy gave her a final, loving look. "Goodbye, Jennifer. Thank you for everything."

With a final surge of energy, the anomaly enveloped Georgiy, and he disappeared from the future. The room was filled with a profound silence as the team processed his departure.

Jennifer stood quietly, tears streaming down her face, but she felt a renewed sense of purpose. Georgiy's legacy would live on through their work, and she was determined to honor his memory by continuing to push the boundaries of science and innovation.

As the IISF entered a new era, inspired by Georgiy's vision, Jennifer and the team found strength in their shared mission. They were united by the memory of a man who had shown them the true meaning of dedication and hope.

Chapter 44

The anomaly's stability fluctuated, and despite their best efforts, the team realized they could not stop the inevitable. Georgiy would have to return to his own time. The atmosphere in the IISF headquarters was somber as the team prepared for his departure.

In the central atrium, the team gathered to say their goodbyes. The room was filled with the quiet murmur of conversations and the soft sounds of people trying to hold back tears. Georgiy stood with Jennifer by his side, both of them trying to savor every last moment together.

Dr. Li stepped forward, his face a mix of sadness and pride. "Georgiy, your contributions to our work and our lives have been immeasurable. We will carry forward your vision and honor your legacy."

Georgiy nodded, his voice thick with emotion. "Thank you, Dr. Li. Working with all of you has been the greatest honor of my life. I have seen a future filled with hope and innovation, and I know you will make it a reality."

Dr. Fernandez and Dr. Moreno approached, their expressions reflecting the deep bond they had formed with Georgiy. "You've been an inspiration to us all," Dr. Fernandez said. "We will continue to build on the foundation you've helped create."

Dr. Moreno added, "Your passion and dedication have driven us to new heights. We will never forget what you've done for us."

Georgiy embraced them both, feeling the weight of their words. "I will carry these memories with me always. Thank you for everything."

As the team members took their turns saying goodbye, Jennifer stood silently by Georgiy's side, her hand tightly clasped in his. When the farewells were nearly complete, she led him to the rooftop garden, the place where they had shared so many moments of peace and reflection.

The stars twinkled above them, a silent witness to their parting. Jennifer turned to Georgiy, her eyes filled with tears. "I don't know how to say goodbye," she whispered. "Every part of me wants to hold on and never let go."

Georgiy gently wiped away her tears, his own eyes shimmering with unshed tears. "This isn't goodbye, Jennifer. Our time together has changed me in ways I can't even begin to describe. No matter where I am, a part of you will always be with me."

She nodded, trying to hold back the sobs that threatened to escape. "I'll never forget you, Georgiy. You've shown me what it means to truly believe in something, to fight for a better future. I promise to carry on your work and keep your legacy alive."

They held each other tightly, the pain of their impending separation almost unbearable. "Remember," Georgiy said softly, "no matter what happens, we've made a difference. And that's something no one can take away from us."

Jennifer nodded, her heart breaking but filled with resolve. "I love you, Georgiy."

"I love you too, Jennifer," he replied, his voice choked with emotion.

As they returned to the atrium, the team gathered around Georgiy one last time. Dr. Li handed him a small device containing all their research and findings. "Take this with you, Georgiy. It's a piece of our future. Use it to continue your work in the past."

Georgiy accepted the device, feeling the weight of its importance. "Thank you. I will use this to build the future we've dreamed of."

The moment had come. The anomaly's energy began to pulse, signaling that the time for Georgiy's departure was near. He stood in the center of the room, the energy swirling around him, as the team watched with heavy hearts.

Jennifer stepped forward, her voice steady but filled with sorrow. "Goodbye, Georgiy. We'll carry your legacy forward."

Georgiy gave her a final, loving look. "Goodbye, Jennifer. Thank you for everything."

With a final surge of energy, the anomaly enveloped Georgiy, and he disappeared from the future. The room was filled with a profound silence as the team processed his departure.

Jennifer stood quietly, tears streaming down her face, but she felt a renewed sense of purpose. Georgiy's legacy would live on through their work, and she was determined to honor his memory by continuing to push the boundaries of science and innovation.

As the IISF entered a new era, inspired by Georgiy's vision, Jennifer and the team found strength in their shared mission. They were united by the memory of a man who had shown them the true meaning of dedication and hope.

Chapter 45

The room was heavy with emotion as the energy of the anomaly enveloped Georgiy. The swirling vortex of light and sound intensified, and the team watched with bated breath, knowing this was the last time they would see him.

Jennifer stood at the front of the group, her eyes locked on Georgiy's. She wanted to remember every detail of this moment, to carry it with her as a source of strength and inspiration.

Georgiy gave the team one final look, his face a mixture of sadness and resolve. "Thank you, everyone," he said, his voice steady despite the whirlwind around him. "Carry on our work. Make the future we dreamed of a reality."

As the vortex reached its peak, Georgiy disappeared, leaving behind a faint echo of light. The room fell silent, the air charged with the weight of his departure.

For a moment, no one moved. The reality of Georgiy's absence settled over them like a heavy blanket. The man who had inspired them, led them through countless challenges, and become a dear friend was gone.

Jennifer felt a deep ache in her chest, a void that seemed impossible to fill. She took a deep breath, trying to steady herself. "We have to keep moving forward," she said softly, her voice trembling but determined. "Georgiy wouldn't want us to stop now."

Dr. Li stepped forward, placing a reassuring hand on her shoulder. "You're right, Jennifer. We need to honor his legacy by continuing our work. He gave us a vision of the future, and it's up to us to make it a reality."

The team nodded in agreement, their faces reflecting a mix of grief and resolve. They knew the path ahead would be challenging, but they were united in their mission.

Over the next few days, the IISF headquarters was a hive of activity. The team threw themselves into their work, finding solace in their shared purpose. Jennifer took on a leadership role, her determination driving the team forward.

Despite the constant buzz of activity, Jennifer found moments of quiet reflection. She would often retreat to the rooftop garden, the place where she and Georgiy had shared so many moments. The stars above seemed to hold a special significance now, a reminder of the man who had touched all their lives.

One evening, as she stood alone in the garden, Dr. Fernandez approached her. "How are you holding up?" he asked gently.

Jennifer sighed, her eyes still fixed on the stars. "It's hard, Dr. Fernandez. I miss him every day. But I know we have to keep going. For Georgiy."

Dr. Fernandez nodded, his expression understanding. "He believed in you, Jennifer. We all do. You're doing an incredible job leading the team."

She turned to him, a small smile on her lips. "Thank you. That means a lot. We've been through so much, and we've come out stronger because of it. I just hope I can live up to the example Georgiy set."

"You already are," Dr. Fernandez said, his voice filled with sincerity. "We're all in this together. And we'll continue to make him proud."

The team's dedication began to bear fruit. Their research progressed rapidly, and they made significant strides in understanding and harnessing the power of the temporal anomaly. Each success felt like a tribute to Georgiy, a testament to the foundation he had helped build.

Jennifer's leadership was instrumental in their progress. She pushed herself and the team to new heights, driven by the memory of Georgiy's passion and vision. Her strength and determination inspired everyone around her, creating a renewed sense of purpose.

One day, as the team celebrated another breakthrough, Dr. Li gathered them for a moment of reflection. "We've achieved so much, and it's all because of the hard work and dedication each of you has shown. Georgiy's legacy lives on in our achievements, and I know he would be proud of what we've accomplished."

Jennifer felt a surge of pride and gratitude. "We have a long way to go, but we're on the right path. Let's continue to honor Georgiy by pushing the boundaries of what's possible and making the future we dreamed of a reality."

As the team raised their glasses in a toast, Jennifer felt a sense of peace. The journey ahead would be filled with challenges, but she knew they had the strength and unity to overcome them. Georgiy's legacy was alive and well, and they were ready to carry it forward into a new era of innovation and discovery.

Chapter 46

Georgiy blinked, disoriented, as the world came into focus. He was back on the plane, seated in the same seat where his extraordinary journey had begun.

He glanced around, taking in the familiar surroundings. The passengers were engaged in quiet conversations, reading books, or watching in-flight movies. It was as if nothing had changed, as if the incredible events he had experienced were nothing more than a vivid dream.

Georgiy rubbed his temples, trying to shake off the lingering sense of disorientation. The future he had seen, the people he had met, and the breakthroughs they had achieved seemed to fade from his memory, like the remnants of a half-remembered dream. Yet, there was a lingering sense of purpose, an inexplicable drive that filled his heart.

He looked out the window at the vast expanse of clouds below, feeling a surge of inspiration. Though he couldn't recall the specifics of his time in the future, he felt a deep-seated conviction that he was meant to achieve something great, something that would shape the world for the better.

Georgiy took a deep breath, his mind racing with possibilities. He couldn't shake the feeling that he had been given a glimpse of what could be, and it was up to him to make that vision a reality. The future was not set in stone; it was a canvas waiting for him to paint with the colors of his inventions and discoveries.

As the plane continued its journey, Georgiy pulled out his notebook and began to scribble down ideas. His pen moved with a newfound urgency, capturing thoughts and concepts that seemed to flow from some hidden wellspring of inspiration. He sketched designs for new technologies, outlined research projects, and jotted down notes on potential collaborations.

He couldn't explain the source of this sudden clarity, but he didn't question it. All he knew was that he had a mission, a purpose that transcended the ordinary bounds of time and space. Georgiy's heart swelled with determination as he vowed to dedicate himself fully to his work, to push the boundaries of science and innovation in ways he had never imagined before.

As the plane began its descent, Georgiy looked out the window one last time, a sense of calm washing over him. He was ready to face whatever challenges lay ahead, armed with the knowledge that he had the power to shape the future. The journey he had embarked on, whether real or imagined, had left an indelible mark on his soul.

Georgiy smiled to himself, feeling a renewed sense of purpose and inspiration. The future was a vast expanse of possibilities, and he was ready to explore it with all the passion and dedication he possessed.

No matter where his path led, he knew that he was destined to make a difference.

Chapter 47

Georgiy's return to the past felt surreal, but he quickly settled back into his routine. He found solace in his work, channeling his energies into his research with a newfound fervor. Though the vivid memories of the future had faded, an unshakable sense of purpose remained, guiding his every step.

Every morning, Georgiy woke up early, his mind buzzing with ideas. He spent hours in his laboratory, surrounded by blueprints, notes, and prototypes. The walls were lined with sketches and equations, each one representing a piece of his vision for the future.

One day, as he tinkered with a new device, his assistant, Anya, walked in. "You've been working non-stop, Georgiy. Don't you ever take a break?"

Georgiy looked up, smiling. "I can't afford to slow down, Anya. There's so much to do, and I feel like I'm running out of time."

Anya frowned. "Running out of time? You've got plenty of it. Just don't forget to take care of yourself."

Georgiy nodded, appreciating her concern. "I know, but I can't shake this feeling. It's like there's something I need to accomplish, something that will change everything."

Despite the challenges and obstacles he faced, Georgiy's determination never wavered. He applied for patents, sought funding for his projects, and collaborated with other scientists, all while pushing the boundaries of what was possible.

One evening, as he reviewed his latest findings, Georgiy felt a sense of déjà vu. The details were hazy, but he knew he was on the right track. His inventions were becoming more advanced, more aligned with the future he had glimpsed.

The sense of urgency that drove him was both exhilarating and exhausting. Georgiy worked late into the night, fueled by a desire to see his vision come to life. His mind was a whirlwind of ideas, each one bringing him closer to the future he could almost remember.

Chapter 48

Back at the IISF, the organization had transformed under Jennifer's leadership. The team, inspired by Georgiy's vision and Jennifer's unwavering dedication, pushed the boundaries of science and innovation.

Jennifer walked through the bustling halls of the IISF headquarters, her mind filled with plans and projects. She paused at a display case, which held a photograph of Georgiy and a plaque commemorating his contributions. It was a reminder of the man who had inspired them all.

In the conference room, Jennifer joined a meeting with her top scientists. They discussed their latest achievements, from breakthroughs in medical technology to advancements in space exploration. The energy in the room was palpable, a testament to their collective drive and passion.

Dr. Li presented a report on their newest project, a revolutionary energy source that promised to change the world. "We're on the verge of something incredible, Jennifer. Georgiy's ideas laid the foundation, and we're building on it every day."

Jennifer nodded, pride swelling in her chest. "He would be so proud of all we've accomplished. Let's continue to honor his legacy by pushing forward, by never settling for anything less than extraordinary."

After the meeting, Jennifer returned to her office and sat at her desk, looking out over the city. The sun was setting, casting a warm glow over the skyline. She thought of Georgiy, of the journey they had shared and the future they had dreamed of.

She picked up a pen and began to write in her journal, reflecting on the impact Georgiy had on her life and the world. "Your vision and your love have guided me, Georgiy. We've faced so much, but we've come through stronger. I promise to continue our work, to make the world a better place, just as you envisioned."

As she wrote, Jennifer felt a sense of peace and purpose. The challenges ahead were daunting, but she knew they could overcome them. The IISF was more than an organization; it was a family, united by a shared mission and inspired by a legacy that would never fade.

Jennifer's leadership brought the IISF into a new era of exploration and discovery. The team's dedication and innovation led to groundbreaking advancements in various fields. One of the most notable projects was the development of a sustainable energy source that could revolutionize the way the world consumed power.

Dr. Fernandez, now one of Jennifer's closest advisors, approached her with an update. "We've completed the final tests on the energy project. The results are beyond our expectations. This could truly change the world."

Jennifer smiled, her eyes lighting up with excitement. "Georgiy's dream was to create a better future, and we're making that dream a reality. Let's prepare for a public announcement. The world needs to know what we've achieved."

The announcement of the new energy source garnered global attention. Leaders from around the world reached out to the IISF, eager to collaborate and implement the revolutionary technology. Jennifer stood at the forefront, guiding her team with confidence and vision.

In the months that followed, the IISF continued to break new ground. They launched initiatives in healthcare, environmental sustainability, and space exploration. Each project was a testament to the innovative spirit that Georgiy had instilled in them.

One evening, Jennifer found herself back in the rooftop garden, the place where she and Georgiy had shared so many moments of reflection and inspiration. The stars twinkled above, a reminder of the vast possibilities that lay ahead.

She sat on a bench, her thoughts drifting to Georgiy. "We've come so far, Georgiy. Your vision and your love have been my guiding light. I wish you could see all that we've accomplished, all that we're still going to achieve."

As she gazed at the stars, Jennifer felt a sense of Georgiy's presence beside her. It was as if he were still with her, guiding her every step of the way. She smiled, feeling a warmth in her heart.

"We'll keep pushing forward," she whispered. "We'll honor your legacy and continue to make the world a better place. Together, we can achieve anything."

With renewed determination, Jennifer stood and looked out at the horizon. The future was bright, filled with endless possibilities. The journey they had started together was far from over, and she was ready to lead her team into a new era of discovery and innovation.

As the night sky enveloped the world, Jennifer felt a profound sense of hope and purpose. Georgiy's legacy lived on through their work, and she was confident that they would continue to make history, one breakthrough at a time.

The IISF's impact on the world grew exponentially under Jennifer's leadership. They were not only at the forefront of scientific discovery but also champions of humanitarian efforts, using their advancements to improve lives across the globe. The vision that Georgiy had sparked became a beacon of hope and progress.

Jennifer often reflected on the journey that had brought her to this point. From the moment she met Georgiy to their time together in the future, every step had shaped her into the leader she had become. She carried his teachings and their shared experiences with her, using them to inspire and guide her team.

One day, as she was reviewing a new project proposal, Jennifer received a message from Dr. Li. "Jennifer, you need to see this."

She walked to the lab, where Dr. Li was waiting with a holographic projection of their latest findings. "We've made a significant breakthrough in our research on temporal anomalies. It's a continuation of Georgiy's work, and it has the potential to unlock even greater possibilities."

Jennifer watched the projection, her heart swelling with pride and excitement. "This is incredible, Dr. Li. Georgiy's legacy continues to inspire us. Let's move forward with this project and see where it leads."

As they worked on the new project, Jennifer felt a renewed connection to Georgiy. His influence was woven into the fabric of their work, a constant reminder of the love and vision that had brought them together.

Years later, Jennifer stood in front of a new generation of IISF scientists. She shared the story of Georgiy and the incredible journey they had undertaken. "Georgiy Garbuz was a visionary, a man who believed in the power of science to change the world. His legacy lives on in each of you. Never forget the importance of our work and the impact it can have on humanity."

The young scientists listened with rapt attention, inspired by the story of Georgiy and Jennifer's journey. They were eager to contribute to the mission, to be a part of the legacy that had shaped the IISF into what it was today.

As Jennifer concluded her speech, she felt a sense of fulfillment. She had honored Georgiy's memory by continuing their shared mission, and she knew that the future was in good hands.

Walking through the halls of the IISF, Jennifer looked at the photographs and artifacts that told the story of their journey. Each one was a testament to the incredible achievements they had made together.

She paused at the display case that held Georgiy's photograph and the plaque commemorating his contributions. "Thank you, Georgiy," she whispered. "For everything. We'll continue to make you proud."

With a final glance at the photo, Jennifer walked forward, ready to lead her team into a new era of discovery and innovation. The future was bright, and she was confident that they would continue to make history, guided by the legacy of love and vision that Georgiy had left behind.

Chapter 49

I t was a quiet night, and Georgiy was engrossed in his work. The soft glow of the lab's lights illuminated his focused expression as he carefully adjusted a circuit. The world outside was dark and silent, the only sounds the hum of his equipment and the occasional rustle of papers.

Suddenly, a knock on the door broke the tranquility. Georgiy frowned, glancing at the clock. It was well past midnight. Who could be visiting at this hour?

He set down his tools and walked to the door, opening it cautiously. To his astonishment, Jennifer stood on the threshold, her eyes wide with emotion.

"Jennifer?" Georgiy whispered, disbelief and joy mingling in his voice.

Jennifer nodded, tears brimming in her eyes. "It's really me, Georgiy. I had to find you."

Georgiy pulled her into a tight embrace, the reality of the moment overwhelming them both. "How? How did you find me?"

Jennifer smiled through her tears. "It wasn't easy. I had to piece together fragments of our research, follow leads, and trust that our connection would guide me here. And it did."

They moved inside, the lab now feeling warmer and more alive with Jennifer's presence. They sat together, hands clasped, as they shared their extraordinary stories.

"I couldn't stop thinking about you," Jennifer said softly. "Even though I didn't know if I'd ever find you again, I had to try. I couldn't just let you disappear from my life."

Georgiy nodded, his heart full. "I felt the same way. Even when I couldn't remember everything clearly, there was a part of me that knew you were out there, that we were meant to be together."

Their eyes locked, and the intensity of their emotions pulled them closer. Slowly, Georgiy leaned in, and Jennifer met him halfway, their lips brushing in a tender kiss. The world outside ceased to exist as they poured all their love and longing into that single moment.

As the kiss deepened, they moved together, guided by a shared need to bridge the gap that time had placed between them. Their hands roamed gently, exploring familiar and cherished territory. The atmosphere was charged with a mix of passion and reverence, each touch and caress a reaffirmation of their bond.

They made their way to a nearby couch, their movements slow and deliberate. Georgiy's fingers trembled slightly as he unbuttoned Jennifer's shirt, his touch gentle and respectful. She responded in kind, her hands tracing the contours of his back with a tenderness that spoke of their deep connection.

As they undressed, the moment was intimate and profound, filled with an unspoken understanding of their shared journey. They came together in a union that was both physical and emotional, their bodies moving in harmony with a rhythm that felt timeless.

Their lovemaking was a dance of passion and love, not hurried but savored. Each kiss, each touch, was an expression of their devotion and a celebration of their reunion. The lab, once a place of solitary work, became a sanctuary of their love, the walls bearing silent witness to their bond.

Afterward, they lay entwined on the couch, the warmth of their bodies mingling. Jennifer rested her head on Georgiy's chest, listening to the steady beat of his heart. Georgiy stroked her hair gently, his mind filled with thoughts of their future.

"I love you, Jennifer," Georgiy whispered, his voice filled with emotion. "No matter what happens, I'll always love you."

Jennifer looked up at him, her eyes shining with tears of happiness. "I love you too, Georgiy. We've found each other again, and I believe we can face anything together."

They held each other close, the promise of their love giving them strength. The challenges ahead were still daunting, but in that moment, they felt invincible, buoyed by the knowledge that their connection had transcended time and space.

As the night wore on, they drifted into a peaceful sleep, their hearts and minds at ease. The future was uncertain, but they knew they would face it together, their love a beacon guiding them forward.

AFTERWORD

Dear Readers,

Thank you for reading *Time Jump*. This enchanting fantasy story blends real-world projects with the imaginative possibilities we all dream of. Within its pages, you've discovered the love story of Georgiy and Jennifer, a tale that transcends time and leads us into the future.

Our motto, *"Za Detey – For Kids! Za Lyubov – For Love! Live, Make, & Enjoy!"* reflects our mission. We are committed to supporting a potential project that aims to provide grants for foster children to attend space school academies. These children are our future, the blossoming flowers of our lives.

I hope you found joy in reading this book. Every purchase helps fund the research and development of these initiatives. I want to extend my heartfelt gratitude to every reader and supporter.

Your support makes this dream a reality. Because of you, children may have access to free education, and everyone may benefit from free healthcare.

Thank you for being a part of this journey. Together, we can create a brighter future.

Proudly sponsored by GarbuzSpace.com

Za Detey – For Kids!

Za Lyubov – For Love!

Live, Make, & Enjoy!

www.ingramcontent.com/pod-product-compliance
Lightning Source LLC
Chambersburg PA
CBHW060449310726
48977CB00001B/367